OMEGA CITY
THE
FORBIDDEN FORTRESS

OMEGA CITY

THE FORBIDDEN FORTRESS

Diana Peterfreund

BALZER + BRAY

An Imprint of HarperCollins*Publishers*

Balzer + Bray is an imprint of HarperCollins Publishers.

Omega City: The Forbidden Fortress

www.harpercollinschildrens.com

Library of Congress Control Number: 2016950332
ISBN 978-0-06-231088-0

Typography by Carla Weise
17 18 19 20 21 CG/LSCH 10 9 8 7 6 5 4 3 2 1
❖
First Edition

For Kristin

CONTENTS

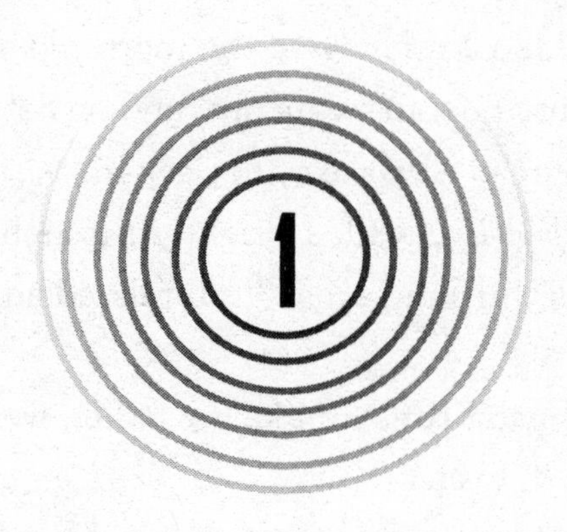

THE FORGOTTEN FORTRESS

I REALLY MISSED MY DAD. THAT WAS THE FIRST THOUGHT THAT CROSSED my mind when my eyes fluttered open to a sunny summer morning. The air was filled with the scent of fresh-baked bread, and I could hear pots and pans rattling in the kitchen of our cottage, but all I wanted to do was shove my head under my pillow and make it all go away.

Instead, I rolled out of bed and shuffled into the living room, which was uncharacteristically spotless. Eric's usual tangle of video game consoles and wires was tucked neatly away, and everything was dusted and buffed to a high shine.

Mom and Eric wore running clothes, which meant

it was Tuesday, Thursday, or Sunday—since Monday, Wednesday, and Friday were the mornings they went to the community pool to swim laps, and on Saturdays, even my mother agreed it was okay to sleep in.

"Hi, Gills!" Eric called brightly through the kitchen door. He was whisking eggs. "You missed a great 5K this morning."

Five-kilometer runs, unlike my father, were not something I missed. Ever.

But Eric's been on a fitness kick. "You never know when you'll have to outrun an exploding rocket ship," he liked to say.

The thing was, we hadn't had to outrun a rocket ship in nearly ten months.

Mom was chopping veggies. "We're making a frittata," she said. "Do you know where your father keeps the cast-iron pan?"

Yes. He'd tossed it after an attempt at pancakes brought the fire department to our door. But there was no way I was going to tattle on him. "Umm . . ."

Mom got that knowing expression on her face anyway. She turned to the pad she'd stuck to the fridge door and added *cast-iron pan* to the growing list there.

I rolled my eyes. That list wouldn't even exist if she hadn't run out on us in the first place. Dad had been on book tour for the past two weeks, and Mom came home from Asia to babysit us.

Before he left, Dad told me I wasn't allowed to call it babysitting, but I don't care. It's not parenting if you're here for less than a month.

"I guess I'm going to make another shopping trip," Mom said. "Gillian, why don't you come along? We can get you some new school clothes."

"I don't need any," I grumbled.

She gave me a small, pained smile and turned to Eric. "Don't whisk too much. You'll bruise the eggs." Then she looked back at me. "Gillian, dear, may I see you in private for a moment?"

Eric shot me a look, then pretended to be fascinated by the bubbles in his bowl.

She brushed past me and down the hall, and I stomped along behind her, fuming. Did she honestly think that lecturing me in another room was somehow saving my dignity? Eric wasn't stupid—he knew I was being dragged off to get in trouble.

Mom ushered me into Dad's office, then shut the door. This was the only room in the house that, so far, had been safe from Mom's influence. She hadn't dared to touch Dad's towering piles of books, notes, photos, and old film reels. But don't give her too much credit. It's not that she didn't want to, it's just that, unlike the kitchen or the living room, it was tough to know where to start without ruining Dad's secret organizational system.

Her expression was one of motherly concern as she crossed her arms over her chest. Behind her, on either side of the door, were eight-foot stacks of Dad's new book, *The Forgotten Fortress.* The black and electric blue of the cover nearly matched her turquoise running outfit and smooth black ponytail.

I matched her stance, crossed arms and all, and stared back at her. "Go ahead and give me that oh-so-important private information about what school clothes I need."

Mom raised her eyebrows. "Gillian, you're almost thirteen. Did you want me to talk about bras in front of your little brother?"

I felt my face heating. *Bras?*

She sighed. "Kiddo, I know it's rough that I haven't been here. Believe me, I wouldn't have gone to Asia if there'd been another option. But there weren't a lot of universities that would have me after . . ." She gestured at Dad's desk. "Well."

After the destruction of Dad's academic reputation and, by association, hers. Both Mom and Dad were history professors, but Dad's controversial research had gotten the whole family in trouble. Ever since the scandal, it had been tough for either of them to find teaching work. Mom had spent the last year studying foot binding in China and pretending she had never married him.

So what if she couldn't get a real job in this country? Dad had made it work—teaching part-time classes at the VA Hall and the occasional seminar to his kooky conspiracy theorist friends. And now he was back, better than ever, with a book that was putting his name on the map.

Thanks to us.

"But I'm here now, and I have a great offer from a school in Idaho. I've been trying to find a time to tell you, but you've been avoiding me since I got here. Eric is really excited about the idea."

"About you living in Idaho?" Why, because it was only half as far away as China?

"About *us* living in Idaho," Mom said.

What? I couldn't have heard that right.

"With your father doing all this visiting lecturing, you guys are going to need something steady. And it would give us the chance to get to know each other again." She looked at me like I had the option to say no, but I knew I didn't. My parents were supposed to split time with us, according to what their lawyers agreed when they got divorced.

And that meant I was moving to Idaho. Getting a bra and moving to Idaho. This was the worst day of my life.

She spread her arms like I was supposed to hug her. I just sniffed and turned around.

"Okay," she said, and I heard another sigh. "I'm going to figure out breakfast. We can maybe do omelets or something. I trust your father didn't ruin the griddle?"

He totally had, in an ill-fated grilled-peanut-butter-sandwich incident.

"Come on out when you're ready, and we'll chat more about it. I made fresh-squeezed orange juice."

Of course she had. Everything with Mom was just *perfect.*

I heard the door close behind her, and then a soft thump. I turned around to find one of the copies of *The Forgotten Fortress* had fallen off the stack.

I picked it up, flipping open the cover to the dedication page.

To Gillian, Eric,
Savannah,
Howard, and Nate.
Without whom
Omega City would have remained buried.

Exactly. If Dad's career was going well now, if the family reputation was improved enough that Mom was getting tenure-track offers in Idaho, then it was because of Omega City, which meant it was because of what *we* did. Me, and Eric, and our friends.

We found the clues in Dr. Underberg's diary that led to the secret entrance. *We* followed them and went into the lost, half-drowned bunker city that was Dr. Underberg's lifework. *We* got chased by thieves and risked our lives and proved that Dr. Underberg wasn't some crazy old scientist.

Well not *just* some crazy old scientist, anyway. Everything in Dad's book was based on the information we'd uncovered. And now Mom wanted to move Eric and me to Idaho? What would Dad do without us? He was still researching his new book on the Arkadia Group, the secret organization that had buried Omega City and threatened anyone—from Dr. Underberg to my father—who tried to expose them. What would happen if we left him alone?

I knew my dad. When he was deep into his research, he sometimes forgot to eat.

I glanced up at the piles of paper still littering Dad's desk, trying to imagine how chaotic it would get, and saw the message light beeping on his office phone. This was exactly what I meant. Dad was terrible at checking messages on the road, with no one to remind him.

I pressed play.

Good afternoon, my name is Dani Alcestis, and I'm calling on behalf of Elana Mero and the Guidant Technologies Foundation. This message is for Dr. Sam Seagret. Ms. Mero is very interested in—

Eric chose that moment to barge in. "Gills, Mom says breakfast is on the table—"

"Shh!"

—your children to the Guidant campus at Eureka Cove to discuss your experiences and potential opportunities for us to learn from one another.

I grabbed a pen and started writing down the phone number on the back of an old map of Area 51.

"What's going on?" Eric whispered, but I'm sure he could hear the message as well as me. The Guidant Foundation was inviting Dad to speak at their high-tech campus—and not just Dad. Us, too, as "participants in the Omega City adventure."

I wonder if that meant Savannah and Howard and Nate, too?

I hopped up and down in excitement as I finished jotting down the message. This was perfect. Dad had been all over the country promoting his book, but clearly these Guidant people had actually read it and realized the part that we kids had played in bringing Omega City to light. This was the first time anyone had bothered asking *us* to talk.

If we started joining Dad at his lectures, then there was no way we could move to Idaho. Dad would need us to stay close, so he could bring us to his events. I imagined standing in front of a crowd of people and talking about scuba diving though an underwater parking lot and up a flooded elevator shaft. I pictured Howard on a stage in his silver Omega City utility suit.

Or maybe we'd all be wearing them. Would they want us to bring them along?

"We have to call her back!" I said when the message finished playing. "This will be awesome for Dad. And us."

"Guidant," said Eric, impressed. "The tech company? Why would they want to talk to Dad?"

"Um, because he's a genius?" Guidant was a huge technology firm. They made computers, software, apps, phones . . . and probably a lot of other stuff. Eric would know better than me.

"But he's a history professor," Eric corrected. "Well, *ex*–history professor." Still, he looked thoughtful. "I heard that if you work for Guidant, your whole family moves onto their property. They call them tech campuses."

"Like university housing?" Even when Mom and Dad had still been married and teaching at the same university, they hadn't wanted to live in the professional housing the school provided. Mom had called it "substandard."

Then again, Mom hadn't yet known how bad it could get, like Dad forcing us all "off grid"—camping in a tent for weeks on end to protect us when the scandal first broke.

That's what had really pushed Mom over the edge.

"Well, that's it, then," I exclaimed. "Omega City is the original tech campus!"

"True," Eric said, though he didn't sound too sure. "Are you sure they want him to lecture? Maybe they want a better battery for their laptops—Underberg's battery."

I held the phone in both hands, hesitating for a moment. Well, Dad could figure that part out, right? I started punching in numbers.

"Wait!" Eric yanked the phone out of my hands. "*You* can't call them back."

"Yes I can," I cried, and grabbed it back. "They invited us, too."

Mom poked her head in the door. "Guys? Cold eggs are the worst. Come on out."

I hid the receiver behind my back. This was none of her business. She didn't have anything to do with Omega City.

But Eric didn't seem to realize this. "Dad just got an invite to the Guidant campus at Eureka Cove," he announced. "And they wanted to know if we could come, too. You know, all us kids. All expenses paid."

Mom smiled. "Really? What an exciting opportunity! After breakfast, we'll call your father and see if he can work it into his schedule."

Eric gave me a smug look. Mama's boy. I watched him

hand my notes over to Mom, then trudged after them as they headed back into the dining room. Silently, I took my place at the table, trying not to enjoy the aroma of fresh bread, melted cheese, and spicy sausage. Breakfast looked delicious. Blecch.

"This could be such a fun vacation for you," Mom was saying as she filled my glass with fresh-squeezed orange juice and handed me a new linen napkin. "Especially if we can get permission from your friends' parents to take them along. Won't that be wonderful? A big last trip with your friends before you move away."

She *would* bring that up. Just when everything was going so well, too.

HIGH (TEMPERATURE) FASHION

"DO YOU THINK YOUR MOM WOULD DO MY COLORS NEXT?" SAVANNAH asked, standing in front of the mirror on my closet door and holding up my new purple dress.

I sat on my bed, surrounded by piles of new school clothes and, yes, three training bras. Mom had finally forced me to go shopping. "You look good in everything," I said.

"No," she replied with a laugh, and grabbed the edge of my utility suit from where it hung in the back, behind my old Easter dresses. "I look awful in silver, remember?"

"Utility suits are hardly high fashion," I pointed out.

"Tell that to Howard. You know I saw him sweating

through that thing four different times this summer down at the baseball fields?"

"What was he doing at the baseball fields?" I asked.

She gave me a look. "Gee, I don't know, Gillian. Golf?"

"I didn't know he played baseball," I said. When had everyone gotten so sporty? First my brother and running, and now Howard?

"The team's called the Rockets," Savannah said. "Maybe he got confused."

That sounded far more likely. As far as I knew, Howard had one interest and one interest only: outer space, and the means of getting there. He'd very nearly headed into orbit with Dr. Underberg last fall.

Savannah rooted around my closet for another minute, then pulled out a green blouse. "This stuff is kind of fancy for school, don't you think?"

I pretended to be very busy examining the fastenings on my stupid new training bra. I still hadn't managed to tell her about Idaho. I was hoping for some kind of last-minute miracle. "My mom picked it out." And what would she know about what I liked to wear?

"Well, your mom has excellent taste," Savannah said. "Isn't it nice to have her back?"

"No." I tore the tag off a sweater. A thick, Idaho-friendly sweater.

Savannah slipped the shirt off the hanger and over her

head. "I'm starting to worry about you, Gillian. I know if my dad ever bothered to come back to town, I'd be glad to see him."

I had no idea why. Savannah had never even met her father. He didn't know what he'd missed by walking out on her mother before she was born. Whereas Mom supposedly loved us, and she still left. Now she thought she could just come back, babysit us for a couple of weeks, then drag us away from Dad and Savannah and everyone else to go to Idaho?

"I don't trust her," I said. "She's not one of us anymore."

"*Us* and *them* again?" Savannah asked. "She's not Fiona."

"She's not *Fiona*?" I spluttered. "That's the best you can do?" The last time I'd seen my father's evil ex-girlfriend, Fiona, she'd been covered in ash, completely deaf, and had just tried to blow up Omega City and trap us underground forever. The woman had been a member of the Arkadia Group, for Pete's sake! No, my mother was not Fiona. That didn't mean we were best friends.

"Well," said Savannah, pulling out another dress from my stack and primping in the mirror. "You should be nice to her anyway. She's driving us all up to the Guidant campus to meet Dr. Mr. Seagret. If you get grounded, it'll ruin the whole weekend."

That was true. The Guidant campus was an hour and a half east, and Mom had offered to drive Eric and me as well as Savannah, Howard, and Nate out there. But I was pretty sure Nate, Howard's seventeen-year-old brother, was only coming because Guidant was just a short bus ride away from one of the colleges he was looking at.

"She can't ground me if she's leaving," I argued. "She won't be home to babysit."

There was a knock on the door and Mom peeked in. "Oh, Savannah, that looks very nice on you."

"Thanks, Dr. Mrs. Seagret!" Savannah beamed at her reflection, shaking out her long blond hair, which, thanks to the summer and copious amounts of lemon juice, was even lighter than usual.

"I just put lunch on the table," Mom said. "We're having ham sandwiches."

Savannah made a face. "Didn't Gillian tell you I'm a vegetarian now?"

"Oh." Mom looked disappointed. "Well, we have cheese. Let me get you some cheese."

Savannah bopped down the hall and I followed. Why was everyone so ready to fit Mom back into their lives? Cheese sandwiches and training bras did not make up for walking out on us when everything fell apart.

We joined Eric at the table while Mom retrieved some

extra swiss cheese for Savannah. I looked at the spread before us with dismay. It was like she was fattening us up for something. Why did everything she served have to look so delicious?

"So, what inspired your vegetarianism?" Mom asked my friend as she sat down.

Eric piled ham on his sandwich. "Her eternal quest for attention?"

Savannah glared at him. "Actually, I read some articles—"

"About vegetarian movie stars—" my brother interrupted.

"Eric!" I cried.

"Well, yes, they were about movie stars," Savannah admitted. "But they were also about the terrible conditions in factory farms, and how much pollution the meat industry causes. Anyway, after I read that—"

"You wanted to be just like them!" Eric clasped his hands under his chin and batted his eyelashes.

"I wanted to take more personal responsibility for what I eat," Sav said smoothly, as if he hadn't spoken. "If Omega City taught me anything, it's that we only have one Earth to live on, so we have to treat it as well as we can so we never actually have to take shelter in a place like that."

"What a wonderful sentiment," said Mom.

Savannah looked at Eric and stuck out her tongue. He took a big bite of his meaty sandwich.

"You should share that story with the Guidant people next week," Mom said.

Our trip was all set. Mom was driving the five of us kids to meet Dad at the Guidant campus in Eureka Cove for the weekend. We'd be taking a tour of their facilities, talking to the engineers about the things we'd seen in Omega City, and even having a special dinner with the Guidant CEO, Elana Mero, herself.

"In fact," she went on, "maybe each of you should work on a little statement about what your trip underground taught you."

That was a great idea. Darn it.

"There were a lot of things that I felt like I lost in the last few years," Eric said. I winced. "Like sailing and scuba diving. But when I was in Omega City, I realized that I still knew how to do those things, and I was glad that I had those skills when I needed them. Now I just want to be ready for whatever comes along."

My sandwich felt like cardboard in my mouth. Exploding rocket ships, indeed.

"What about you, Gillian?" Mom made the mistake of asking.

I put my sandwich back on my plate. "What I learned

is that it's important to believe that Dad knows exactly what he's talking about, even if everybody else has abandoned him."

Everyone at the table fell silent. Mom put her sandwich down and wouldn't meet my eyes. "Excuse me . . ." She left the table. A few seconds later, I heard her door shut.

"Gillian!" Eric kicked me under the table. Hard. "What's wrong with you?"

"What's wrong with *me*?" I asked, incredulous. "What's wrong with you? You were just as mad at her last year as I was! And now it's all 5Ks and swimming lessons and moving to Idaho."

"What?" Savannah asked. "What's this about Idaho?"

"I was mad," Eric said, "because she was *gone*. But now she's *back*."

"Oh, great!" I threw my hands up in the air. "All's forgiven! Hey, Fiona hasn't tried to kill us in ten months, is she okay now, too?"

"Mom," Eric said in a dangerous whisper, "is *not* Fiona."

Savannah nodded. "I'm with Eric on that one. I can't believe you, Gillian."

"Fine!" I pushed away from the table. "I'm used to not being believed." I stomped outside. On the porch, our cat Paper Clip was snoozing on the glider, her striped yellow tail flicking lazily back and forth.

She was a traitor, too. One woven ball filled with catnip and the cat was Mom's slave. And I loved Paper Clip, but honestly, that kind of behavior was enough to make me agree with Dad that felines were completely untrustworthy.

I paced the porch, bristling. No one followed me outside. No one did anything. Some best friend. Some brother.

Some mom.

One week until I saw Dad again. He would understand what I was going through. He wouldn't be all hunky-dory with Mom just because she never burned our dinner and knew how to run a vacuum and liked to jog at sunrise and bought me school clothes.

Maybe he would even insist we couldn't move. Maybe Dad would see how helpful we were at Guidant and want us to come to more of his events. I had to be here, to encourage Dad with his next book . . . and make sure he didn't light the kitchen cabinets on fire while brewing coffee.

Though, to be fair, that had only happened once.

I hopped on my bike and sped off down the dirt road leading to our cottage. Clearly, Savannah and Eric weren't on my side. I needed to hang out with people who would be. And that meant I needed the Nolands.

BY THE TIME I got to Nate and Howard's house, the August sun had turned my ponytail into a frizzy mess and made my shirt stick to my skin. I stood on their front porch, wiping streaks of road dust off my face with the back of my sweaty hand.

"Gillian," said Mrs. Noland, when she came to the door. "What a surprise. Are the boys expecting you?"

"No, ma'am," I replied. "Are they home?"

"Nate's got a shift at the pool," Mrs. Noland said. "But Howard's out back"—she hesitated—"testing a hypothesis. He says."

Right. Of course. "Should I go around?"

She pushed open the screen. "Come through the kitchen. You look like you could use some lemonade."

I probably looked like I could use a whole bath of lemonade. In the kitchen, Mrs. Noland loaded up a tray with two glasses, a tall pitcher of water for the lemonade, and a bowl of pretzels.

"We haven't seen you much this summer," she said as she stirred the pink lemonade mix into the water. "Of course, Howard's been so busy with the baseball team. Have you been to any of the games?"

"No," I admitted. "Howard didn't mention he'd started playing."

Mrs. Noland looked at me. "Oh, he doesn't play, dear. He runs the stats."

"Oh." That made more sense.

"Anyway, the boys are so excited about the trip next

week. Ask your mother to take lots of pictures. I think it'll be great for Nate's college applications, that he's giving advice to engineers at Guidant. I've already told him he should write his application essay about Omega City."

"Okay," I said. Did that mean Mom was staying for the whole thing? That wasn't supposed to be part of the deal.

I headed out to the backyard, loaded down with the tray. The heat out here was even worse than it had been on the ride over, as the tall fence seemed to keep out even the breeze. Howard's yard was totally devoid of trees, and the sky was a bright, solid blue. I spotted Howard right away, or at least, a Howard-shaped object. He was lying perfectly still on a vinyl chaise longue in the middle of the yard, encased head to foot in his Omega City utility suit. Even his hood was up.

I hurried over as quickly as my tray of dishes and lemonade would allow. He was going to get heatstroke in that thing.

"Howard!" I cried. "Are you all right?" I put the tray down on the side table. There was a solar-powered radio there, tuned to some news channel.

"Yes," came his voice from inside the dark visor. "Is that lemonade?"

"Yeah." He sounded so calm.

"What color?"

"Um, pink?"

He sat up and unzipped the hood, pulling it down around his face. "That's the only drawback of this thing," he said. "The dark visor really distorts the visible spectrum."

I stared at him, openmouthed. I'd expected him to look like he'd just stepped out of a steam room, dripping with sweat in the hot summer sun. But he seemed nice and cool.

Howard was examining the contents of the pitcher. "I hope she remembered to account for the dilution of melted ice in the mixture this time. But at least it's pink."

"You only drink pink lemonade?" Howard had a lot of weird rules about food, and none of them, unlike Savannah's, were based on what he'd read in a celebrity magazine.

I might be mad at Eric, but he was totally right about the vegetarianism.

"If it's from a mix, I only drink pink," he said. "If it's real, I won't drink pink, because they make it with strawberries."

"So why do you only drink pink from a mix?"

He frowned. "I won't drink pink if it's real." As if that made sense.

I still wasn't sure I understood, but I poured us some lemonade anyway. On the radio, a news announcer was talking about a newly discovered comet. "So what's your hypothesis? Your mom said—"

"Shh!" Howard turned up the volume. "I want to hear this."

"—Capella satellite, designed to detect and monitor near-Earth objects, will be assisting NASA when the comet passes within three hundred thousand miles of Earth this month. This will be the closest space object to pass by Earth this decade."

"Wow," said Howard. "That's close."

And Howard would know. Of course, thanks to Howard and Dr. Underberg, I knew all the relative distances, too. The moon was about two hundred and forty thousand miles away. So this comet *was* super close.

The radio announcer started talking about some environmental disaster, and Howard flicked the switch and grabbed a glass of lemonade. "My hypothesis," he said. "I'm testing the cooling functions on the suit. It's twenty degrees in here, at the lowest setting. In Celsius, of course."

"Oh. Cool." Actually, I had no idea what that would be in Fahrenheit, and Savannah wasn't here to do the math for me. But it must be cool. "Wait, is that why you've been wearing your suit to the baseball games?"

"Yes," he replied. "It's hot out there, and the dugout doesn't have any air-conditioning."

I laughed. "Savannah said she thought it was because the team is the Rockets."

"What would that have to do with me wearing an Omega City utility suit?"

"Because it looks like a space . . . never mind." I sat down on the edge of the lounger and put up my hand to try to shade my eyes from the sun. It didn't work so well, especially since Howard's silver suit was bouncing rays all over the yard.

Still, baking alive was better than my house with my mom and her fan club. I knew for sure that Howard would have no interest in my mom. If it wasn't about NASA, he didn't care.

"Are you looking forward to the trip to Guidant?" I asked.

Howard fiddled with the hexagonal zipper pulls on his suit. Their faceted surfaces glittered in the sunlight. "I'm not sure. I think it'll be fun to see the technology on the Guidant campus, and I'm glad that my parents are letting Nate and me go alone, because they've never let us go anywhere without them before. Except Omega City, of course, and they didn't know about that."

No, no one's parents would have let their kids go exploring a drowned underground city. Not even my father.

"But I don't know what they want us to tell them. They have your dad's book. Everything we know about Omega City is already in there."

"There's always more to tell," I said. "That's what Dad does every day. Meets with people who have read his book and tells them more details and lets them ask questions."

Howard hesitated for a moment. "But if he didn't put it in the book, didn't he have a good reason?"

"Like what?"

"Like protecting Dr. Underberg."

"You mean because he tried to get a bunch of kids to run away to outer space with him?" I admit, if you hadn't been there with us, underground, while Omega City was being drowned under water and explosions were rocking the cavern, Dr. Underberg's offer to make room for us in his rocket ship might have struck you as a little . . . odd. Even in the moment, only Howard had considered it—and Nate had to practically beg him to unbuckle himself from his seat on the ship and escape with us.

And it was a good thing, too, since Dad never did find out what had happened to Dr. Underberg after his ship took off.

I wasn't a space expert like Howard, but I did know how hard space travel was even on young, healthy astronauts. It had been ten months since *Knowledge* had rocketed into the stratosphere. Even if Dr. Underberg somehow had a fully operational life-support system in place—which was unlikely, given the state of the rest of Omega City—it didn't mean that an eighty-six-year-old man would survive such a voyage.

"No," said Howard. "Not about that. But Dr. Underberg had secrets to keep. What if by talking about Omega City, we accidentally tell them?"

CAKE AND CODE BREAKING

THE DAY BEFORE WE LEFT FOR EUREKA COVE WAS HOWARD'S BIRTHDAY, and his parents invited Savannah, Eric, me, and our moms to come out with them for pizza. Even though we weren't sure if it counted as a birthday party, Mom insisted we bring gifts. She even drove us to the mall to shop, but since the mall didn't have a NASA store, we were sort of at a loss. We wandered up and down the aisles of the toy store, as Mom pointed out Star Wars Lego sets and astronaut ice cream.

"He'd only eat it if it's Omega City brand," Eric said, which was true. And, obviously, the ice cream was not.

"It's not like there's anything space-related that *we'd*

know about but not him," Savannah pointed out as we left the store empty-handed. "The only thing I can think of that Howard might want for his birthday is a ride in a real rocket ship. You know, the one he didn't get in Omega City."

That reminded me of our conversation the other day. After I'd talked with Howard, I'd gone home and read through the sections about us and our adventures in *The Forgotten Fortress*, looking for any important details Dad might have left out, but that wasn't Dad's style. He was the one who found out other people's secrets, and told the whole world.

Still, it was sweet that Howard wanted to protect Dr. Underberg.

"Hey, guys?" Mom had stopped in front of a fancy stationery store. "What about a space pen?" She pointed at a sleek silver object in the window. "This says it was designed by NASA and has been used on all manned missions since 1968. You could go in on it together. They'll even engrave his name on it."

I had to hand it to Mom. That was a pretty good idea. The pen was silver, like a little rocket ship, and came in a box with a NASA seal and certification and everything. We debated for a while about what the engraving should say. At first, we'd all thought *Howard,* but Mom suggested that *H.*

Noland or *Howard Noland* might look "more professional."

"But he's not a professional," I said. "He's a sixth grader."

"I like H. Noland," Savannah said, ignoring me. "It's dignified."

"Yeah," Eric agreed. "Plus, we have to pay by the letter."

We chose a nice block print and the man engraved the pen, and even wrapped it in pretty blue paper with a white ribbon.

As we walked out of the store, Savannah shook her head, grinning. "If you told me a year ago that I'd be spending two hours picking out a present for Howard Noland's birthday, I would have laughed in your face."

"Yeah, especially if I told you that it was an engraved pen, and you agreed with Eric about what the engraving should say."

That made her stop dead in her tracks.

GENERAL TSO'S PIZZA was located in an old brick building that I'm pretty sure used to be a chain pizza place. The roof had an odd, distinctive shape barely camouflaged by the weird dragons and other designs that had been added to the exterior of the building to make it look like a pagoda. Inside, murals of Venetian canals fought with silk screens, and carved wooden Buddhas stood next to plump Italian chefs holding bottles of wine.

"Ah," said Mom with a pained smile. "I'd forgotten how . . . unique this place is. Has the food gotten any better?"

"Nope." Eric smiled and waved at Nate, Howard, and their mother, who were hanging out at one of the four booths lining the walls. The restaurant was empty—most people who ate the food here ordered delivery.

"Hey, guys," said Nate as he dragged over a table to add to the end of the booth for us. We all sat down. "You know what you want?"

"I don't," Mom said. She opened the menu. "Has the waiter been by?"

"Waiter?" said Nate, as if he'd never before heard the word. "Yeah, they don't have one of those. Just tell me what you want and I'll tell the kitchen. I used to work here."

Nate had done delivery for General Tso's, back before his truck got wrecked during the launch of the rocket ship *Knowledge*. This winter, he'd made extra cash by shoveling snow and chopping wood, and this summer, he'd started mowing lawns. He said he liked it way more than delivering pizza.

"Why?" Savannah had asked a few months ago.

And Nate had replied, "Because you don't have a lawn, Savvy," which had made Eric laugh for about five minutes straight.

"Oh," Mom said. "I think I'll try the chicken fried linguini."

"Your funeral," said Nate. He looked at us. "The usual?"

We all nodded, and Nate headed off to the kitchen. I handed Howard our present.

"Thanks," he said, looking at the table. He put it with a small pile of other gifts.

"Thank you for inviting us to your birthday dinner," Mom prompted.

"Yeah, thanks," Eric echoed dutifully.

"Thank you for coming," Mrs. Noland responded. "We're so glad to have some of Howard's friends over."

For once. She didn't say that, but the words seemed to hang in the air until Nate came back to the table with a pitcher of lemonade and a bunch of glasses. "When is Dad getting here?"

"He has to work late tonight," his mother explained, and poured a glass of lemonade. "Here you go, birthday boy. Should we start with the presents?" She reached for a big, oblong one. "This one's from your father."

It was tough for Howard to get the paper off while cornered in the booth. Inside was a baseball bat and a set of two balls, as well as a note.

"'Dear Howie,'" Howard read, his voice flat. "'To help you make the team next summer.'"

I looked up to catch Nate rolling his eyes. I didn't blame him. We all knew how much Howard hated it when his father called him Howie.

"Isn't that nice," said Mrs. Noland, sounding almost as toneless as her son.

Not really. Howard was staring at the bat as if he'd never seen one before.

The table fell silent. Mom cleared her throat and took a long drink of her lemonade. This was officially the most awkward birthday party I'd ever been to.

"Open ours," Savannah suggested. Howard grabbed our package and neatly unwrapped the paper.

"Oh, a space pen," said Howard.

"Yeah," said Eric, smiling. "We got it engraved."

"Thanks," Howard said. He looked at his mom. "Look, you can use this, too. *H. Noland* can stand for Hope."

"That's an awfully fancy pen," Mrs. Noland said.

"It was invented by NASA," Savannah said. "It can write upside down, underwater . . ."

"Wow," said Mrs. Noland.

"NASA spent several years developing this pen in the sixties, so the astronauts could write in zero g," Howard said. "It's been on every manned space mission since its invention."

Savannah and Eric beamed. "We knew you'd like it," Savannah said.

Howard looked at the pen. "But you know what the Russian cosmonauts did?"

"What?" I asked.

"They used a pencil."

Nate spit his lemonade across the table.

"Nathaniel!" his mother said, horrified. "And Howard, that's not how you thank people for gifts."

Mom was trying not to laugh.

"I'm going to go get the food," Nate said, his eyes watering.

"I do like it," Howard said. "There's no such thing as a space pencil."

"You're welcome, Howard," I said. That *was* a thank-you, for him.

Thankfully, Nate came back with a tray of food, and for a while the only thing we talked about was how to divide up the egg-roll calzones and whether sesame chicken pizza was better or worse than kung pao shrimp pizza.

Mom poked at her chicken fried linguini. She really should have known better.

"So, Dr. Seagret," Mrs. Noland said, "Howard tells me you're taking the kids to Idaho in the fall. We'll be sorry to lose them. Howard has grown so close to Eric and Gillian."

Mom stole a glance at me, and maybe it was my imagination, but she almost looked guilty. Yeah, Mom. See? You aren't just taking us away from Dad and my best friend, you're also leaving Howard with no one but his brother and Savannah for company.

And that was assuming Sav and Howard would still hang out once we were gone.

"You tell her, Mrs. N," Savannah said, twirling a fork through her Caprese chow mein. "Gillian's only been here full-time for a year, and now she's going to leave again? That sucks."

"Well, you'll all just have to have as much fun as possible this weekend to make up for it," Mom said. "They've got such lovely facilities at the Guidant campus. And it's on the water, too, so you'll be able to go swimming and water skiing and sailing. . . ." She gave Eric an encouraging smile.

"Not a lot of sailing in Idaho," I added.

Eric kicked me under the table. "Who's the silver one from?" he asked Howard, pointing at a rectangular present.

"I don't know," Howard replied. "It showed up on the doorstep without a card. We think maybe it's from my grandparents. It looks like a book."

"Why don't you open it and see?" Nate asked. "By the way—spoiler alert—I also got you a book."

"Yeah," Howard said. "But you got me that book on the effects of long-term space flight on the body . . . didn't you?"

Nate looked confused. "Wait, was that the one you mentioned five dozen times?"

Howard looked at his brother. Nate waited three seconds before he grinned.

"Oh," said Howard. "You're joking."

"Yeah." Nate bit off a chunk of pizza crust. "Open the other one."

Howard pushed his plate aside and grabbed the silver gift. Inside was a large brown hardcover engraved with a simple gold title, *Codes and Code Breaking.* There was no author listed.

"Cool," said Howard.

We all blinked at him. Cool? What did codes have to do with space travel? Coding, maybe, but I doubt a book that old had any cool computer stuff in it.

"I taught myself Morse code this summer," he said. "You'd think it's obsolete, with the improvement in communication techniques, but I've been thinking a lot about the SETI Institute."

"SETI?" Savannah asked.

"The search for extraterrestrial intelligence," I explained. "They look for aliens."

"They study radio signals for signs of extraterrestrial communication," Howard clarified. "But obviously, extraterrestrials aren't going to communicate in English."

"They aren't going to communicate in Morse code, either," Eric said.

"No," said Howard. "Probably not. But the more I learn about how human languages and codes work, the more prepared I am."

"To talk to aliens?" asked Eric. He looked at me. "This is your doing, isn't it?"

I held up my hands in defense. I had nothing to do with Howard deciding that codes were as cool as the cosmos.

"No, to separate signal from noise. Language has patterns. If you can figure out how the patterns work, you can figure out if it's some kind of message. That's the first thing you learn with code. Look . . ." He flipped the cover of the book open and tapped a page. "It's called frequency analysis. You study the repetition of certain letters or groups of letters to try to break codes."

"Like how in English, E is the most common letter?" Savannah asked.

"Right. And if there is a word with only one letter . . ."

"It's 'I' or 'a,'" Eric finished. "Cool."

"So who gave you this book?" Mrs. Noland asked. "It's not from us. And I know Grandma got you a sweater."

"Check in the front," my mom suggested. "Maybe there's an inscription."

Howard turned to the front of the book. Sketched out in pencil was a square of numbers.

14 43 13 13 45 31 35 14 44
25 11 53 15 43 23 35 11 34
15 35 23 31 21 13 34 31 13
52 13 45 25 31 44 53 31 34
34 44 11 11 35 21 13 51 44
13 24 51 34 45 11 54 11 51
14 11 11 23 34 51 22 33 23
43 15 34 11 54 44 31 51 44
51 35 23 13 43 21 13 43 14

"Weird," Eric said. "Even the inscription is in code."

"Or someone was doing a math problem and needed paper," Savannah said.

But I was staring at the neatly drawn rows of numbers as my slices of sesame chicken pizza turned over and over in my stomach.

Not again. How could they be looking at this writing—how could Howard be looking at it—and not see what I saw?

If those numbers were a code, I had no idea what they meant. But I did know who'd put them there.

Dr. Underberg.

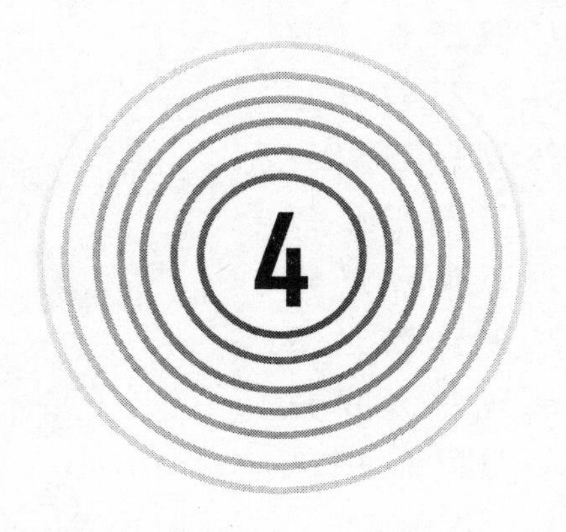

SUB-SUB-SUBORBITAL

I WAS IN A DAZE THROUGH THE REST OF THE MEAL, AS HOWARD OPENED his grandparents' sweater and Nate's book on long-term space travel and the new pair of sneakers from his mom. I barely touched my green tea ice cream sundae.

Maybe I was just imagining it was his handwriting. Dr. Underberg wouldn't send Howard a present. But my birthday wasn't for a month yet, and he hadn't sent Eric one on his. And how could he even send something from outer space, anyway?

But if he had . . . why would it be a book on codes?

After Mom drove us home from General Tso's, Savannah headed back across the creek to finish packing for the trip, Mom went into her room to answer some emails, and as soon as we were alone, I cornered my brother near his room.

"Hey," I said. "Do you think Dad gave away all Dr. Underberg's secrets in his book?"

He shrugged. "I wouldn't know. I never read it."

"You didn't read Dad's book?"

"I *lived* it. Have the fake teeth to prove it and everything." He tapped one of his ceramic incisors. "But yeah, I guess so. I mean, Omega City was his big secret, right? That and the battery."

"But it doesn't say how to make the battery in the book."

"Well," Eric said, "that's because Dad's not an engineer. I figured the battery is what the Guidant people are really interested in, don't you?"

I frowned. Fiona had wanted that battery. So had the Shepherds.

Eric saw my face. "Come on, Gills. That's not a bad thing, just because the bad guys wanted to steal credit for inventing the battery. Dr. Underberg would have wanted *someone* to use it. He was trying to save the world."

"'Would have wanted'?" I echoed. "Do you think he's dead?"

Eric's eyes widened. "I mean . . . I don't know. He was really old and unhealthy and . . ." He frowned. "Why are you asking me about this? Howard is the one with the new book on the long-term effects of space travel."

I took a deep breath. "That's not the only book Howard has. That code-breaking book—I think that was Dr. Underberg's handwriting in the front."

Eric shook his head. "Oh, Gills, not the handwriting thing again."

"Again?" I said defensively. "I was *right* last time."

"He's an old guy. They took penmanship classes and stuff back then, so they all had good handwriting. Maybe you just think it's him because it's an old book and it has fancy handwriting in it."

"What other old man would send Howard a book?"

"From outer space? I have no idea," Eric scoffed. "Besides, it's not even real writing. Just a string of numbers."

"Hey, guys?" Mom's voice floated down the hall. "Don't stay up too late tonight, okay? We've got an early start tomorrow morning. Are you all packed?"

"Yes," we answered in unison.

"Look," Eric said. "What difference does it make if he is floating around up there, sending down birthday presents like a space-age Santa Claus?"

"Well, if he is, then Dad doesn't have the right to give away his battery without his permission. We have to find out."

Eric crossed his arms and gave me a smug glare. "We

do, huh? When? Before tomorrow?"

"Before we give Guidant the battery."

"*We*? A second ago it was Dad."

"Of course it's *we*." After all, I'd been the one to bring the battery out of Omega City in the pocket of my utility suit . . . even though it had been an accident. "That's why we're all going to Guidant."

"Um, no, it's not. I don't know the first thing about how patents or whatever work. But I'm sure Dad has thought this through, even if you haven't." Eric went on. "And here's something else you haven't thought through. If Dr. Underberg is out there, and Guidant or anyone else who might want to talk to him about his inventions could, what makes you think they'd want to talk to Dad . . . or us?"

I clapped my mouth shut.

Eric shook his head, like he was disappointed in me. "So which is it? Is Dr. Underberg out of the picture, or is he around to answer people's questions while we're with Mom in Idaho?"

I clenched my jaw. "This has nothing to do with Mom . . . or Idaho!"

"Sure it doesn't." He rolled his eyes and shut the door to his bedroom, leaving me to make faces at the wood.

I TOSSED AND turned all night, my dreams a mishmash of thick sweaters, crashed rockets, and space pens. I couldn't believe my brother. Sure, I didn't want to move to Idaho. But not so much that I'd rather Dr. Underberg disappeared again . . . or worse.

By the time I woke up, my brain was so foggy I could hardly think of what to pack. Eric and I still weren't speaking to each other, and since I usually did my best not to talk to Mom, either, that meant I spent all of breakfast completely mute. By the time Savannah met us at the van to load up our bags, I felt as gloomy as the overcast sky.

Savannah looked sunny, though—literally, as she wore a pretty yellow dress printed with daisies. And, I noticed, a bra.

She frowned at my old jean shorts and T-shirt. "That's not what you're wearing when we have our meeting, is it?"

"No. I'll change when we get there." Although now I wasn't sure if the khaki pants I'd brought were the right choice, either. When Mom and I had gone shopping the other day, she'd bought me an A-line skirt she suggested I wear at Guidant, but I hadn't packed it. Now I wondered if I should have.

"I forgot something in my room," I shouted, and ran back inside. The skirt was hanging in my closet and I grabbed it and stuffed it into my backpack, hoping that wherever we were staying on the Guidant campus had irons.

"Don't get too excited," Eric was saying when I got

back in the van. He was sitting shotgun. "I bet you a dollar Dad makes us all wear our utility suits when we get there."

"He wouldn't!" Savannah looked at my mom. "Would he?"

Mom chuckled. "He certainly didn't mention anything like that."

"Then why did he make us bring them?" Eric teased.

"For . . . props." Savannah smoothed out her skirt. "Maybe it'll be enough that Howard wears his."

I settled into the middle seat next to Savannah, but we didn't talk much as Mom headed off to pick up the Noland boys. I wanted to tell Sav about my suspicions, but I knew the second I opened my mouth, Eric would start making fun of me again.

Along with his bag, Nate carried an SAT prep book, and Howard—who was, of course, wearing his utility suit—came armed with *Codes and Code Breaking*.

"Oh, are you studying for the SAT, Nate?" Mom asked, looking at him through the rearview mirror.

"Yes, ma'am," Nate replied. "I have to take it again. It's the math that's killing me."

"Have you thought of a tutor?"

"It's next on the list," he mumbled. "If I can't figure out rational and quadratic equations."

Beside me, Savannah twisted her hands in her lap. I'd bet a dollar she was as itchy to get her hands on Nate's SAT prep book as I was to get another look inside *Codes and Code Breaking*. I had an idea.

"Hey, Nate," I said. "Can you switch with me?"

Nate shrugged and we climbed over the backs of the seats. Last year, Savannah would have swooned to have Nate Noland sitting next to her. Now all she wanted to do was check out his calculations.

Once I was buckled in next to Howard, I could see that he had his head bent low over the book. He had a small pad of paper nestled inside the pages, and it was covered in numbers and symbols I couldn't begin to understand.

"So it's pretty good reading?" I asked.

He grunted. The neck of his utility suit was zipped tight, and he was chewing on the zipper pull.

"He was up all last night with it," Nate announced from the middle row. "I think we may have discovered a new obsession."

"You forgot to divide by *x*," Savannah murmured, mostly to herself.

"What?" said Nate, then looked down at his work. "Oh, crud." He started rubbing away his work with the eraser end of his pencil.

I concentrated on Howard. "Can I see the book for a second?"

He spat out the hexagonal zipper pull and said, "Maybe later," which I'm pretty sure meant *absolutely not.* He turned another page, and I caught more telltale scribbles in Dr. Underberg's handwriting. I arched my neck to get a closer peek, and Howard slammed his hand down over the writing.

"Do you mind?" he asked. "If people watch me create my code, then it's not very secret."

I sat back, frowning. "If you aren't going to tell us your code, then who are you making it for?" I was no expert, but I was pretty sure the first lesson in any book on code making was that there was no point in writing coded messages if no one else could break them.

Howard said nothing, and after another minute of sitting in silence, I tried again.

"Did you ever figure out who gave you the book?" I asked. "It's so mysterious."

He stopped writing on the pad. "No, it's not. It was the first code I broke. Turns out it was a simple Polybius square."

"Oh," I said, like I'd heard of those before.

"Chapter one." He flipped to the front of the book. "They're one of the simpler forms of ciphers. Well, easy as long as you can figure out what the keyword is. See, what you do is you make a square out of the alphabet, and then you number the axes, and every number combination conforms to a letter." He showed me the diagram in the book.

	1	*2*	*3*	*4*	*5*
1	*A*	*B*	*C*	*D*	*E*
2	*F*	*G*	*H*	*I*	*J*
3	*K*	*L*	*M*	*N*	*O*
4	*P*	*Q*	*R*	*S*	*T*
5	*U*	*V*	*W*	*Y*	*X/Z*

"Why do they put X and Z together like that?" I asked.

"Because they're rarely used," he replied. "And because usually you will know in a word if it's an X or a Z that you need. Anyway, if you're writing out the code, you'd just use the corresponding horizontal and vertical axis letters to make the numbers. So A would be eleven, and B would be twelve, et cetera."

"Carry the twelve . . . oops," said Nate from in front of us, starting in with his eraser again. "Guys, you're confusing me with all this talk about axes and numbers."

"Yeah," Savannah said under her breath. "*That's* what's confusing you."

Howard dropped his voice to a whisper. "This is a pretty easy code to break."

"It is?" I asked, looking skeptically at the lists of numbers. It didn't look easy to me.

"Well, it is if you know anything at all about codes. I mean, you shouldn't use it in a war or anything, but it helps to make a quick code, or if your messages are extremely short. Also, if you wanted to make it harder to break, you can use a keyword."

"What do you mean?"

It goes at the front of the key and kind of shifts the rest of the alphabet to the side. So say your keyword is 'party' . . ." He pointed to the next graph in the book, where that indeed was the keyword. "You just fill out the graph again, but you put 'party' on the first line, and then you skip all those letters when you get to them in the alphabet."

	1	*2*	*3*	*4*	*5*
1	*P*	*A*	*R*	*T*	*Y*
2	*B*	*C*	*D*	*E*	*F*
3	*G*	*H*	*I*	*J*	*K*
4	*L*	*M*	*N*	*O*	*Q*
5	*S*	*U*	*V*	*W*	*X/Z*

"So then A would be twelve and B would be twenty-one," I pointed out.

"Exactly. Or you could do the alphabet backward or skip all the vowels or whatever. The possibilities are endless, as long as the other person knows—or can guess—the keyword."

Suddenly, I understood why Howard had been up all night with this book. Though he still hadn't answered my question. "So how did you figure out who the book was from?"

"By breaking the coded inscription in the front." He flipped to the very first page of the book, and again I saw the square of numbers from last night. Underneath, in Howard's messy hand, was the translation.

"The hard part," he said, "was figuring out the keyword. I had to try several. Of course, I should have guessed the keyword was 'Omega,' because . . ."

But I had stopped listening, because the answer was right in front of me:

14	*43*	*13*	*13*	*45*	*31*	*35*	*14*	*44*
G	*R*	*E*	*E*	*T*	*I*	*N*	*G*	*S*
25	*11*	*53*	*15*	*43*	*23*	*35*	*11*	*34*
H	*O*	*W*	*A*	*R*	*D*	*N*	*O*	*L*
15	*35*	*23*	*31*	*21*	*44*	*53*	*31*	*13*
A	*N*	*D*	*I*	*B*	*E*	*L*	*I*	*E*
52	*13*	*45*	*25*	*31*	*44*	*53*	*31*	*34*
V	*E*	*T*	*H*	*I*	*S*	*W*	*I*	*L*
34	*44*	*11*	*11*	*35*	*21*	*13*	*51*	*44*
L	*S*	*O*	*O*	*N*	*B*	*E*	*U*	*S*
13	*24*	*51*	*34*	*45*	*11*	*54*	*11*	*51*
E	*F*	*U*	*L*	*T*	*O*	*Y*	*O*	*U*
14	*11*	*11*	*23*	*34*	*51*	*22*	*33*	*23*
G	*O*	*O*	*D*	*L*	*U*	*C*	*K*	*D*

43	*15*	*34*	*11*	*54*	*44*	*31*	*51*	*44*
R	*A*	*L*	*O*	*Y*	*S*	*I*	*U*	*S*
51	*35*	*23*	*13*	*43*	*21*	*13*	*43*	*14*
U	*N*	*D*	*E*	*R*	*B*	*E*	*R*	*G*

Greetings, Howard Noland. I believe this will soon be useful to you. Good luck. Dr. Aloysius Underberg.

WELCOME TO GUIDANT

THE BOOK *WAS* FROM DR. UNDERBERG! I ALMOST SHOUTED, *I TOLD YOU so!* to Eric, all the way up front. But the rest of the message baffled me. What did he mean, this would be useful?

Howard was still speaking. ". . . I tried 'birth,' of course, since it was a birthday present. And 'gift.' But then I thought maybe this had something to do with the puzzle I solved that led to Omega City. You know, the one from Dr. Underberg's treasure map."

As if I could forget. "Why didn't you tell me this was from Dr. Underberg?" I asked.

Howard shrugged. "You didn't ask."

I sighed. Sometimes, he was really impossible. "Okay.

So how did you eventually break the code?"

He shoved the pad under my nose. "I tried 'Omega.' See?"

	1	*2*	*3*	*4*	*5*
1	*O*	*M*	*E*	*G*	*A*
2	*B*	*C*	*D*	*F*	*H*
3	*I*	*J*	*K*	*L*	*N*
4	*P*	*Q*	*R*	*S*	*T*
5	*U*	*V*	*W*	*Y*	*X/Z*

Don't get me wrong; I was impressed by Howard's work, but I was much more interested in knowing how Dr. Underberg had given him the book . . . and why. Was he suddenly going to start pelting us with coded messages from . . . well, wherever in outer space he'd gone to?

No, he must have landed, sometime, somewhere. And if he had, that meant he was safe. No matter what Eric thought, that was still important to me.

This made perfect sense. After all, the Shepherds were still out there, so of course Dr. Underberg would want to stay in hiding. Maybe he planned to communicate with us through code.

I believe this will soon be useful . . . Maybe he could tell us what he wanted us to do with the battery! Of course! *We* were the ones he trusted, not Guidant. Not even Dad.

Howard was now talking about Playfair ciphers and the difference between those and something called a straddling checkerboard. I stopped him in the middle of a whole explanation on fractionation. Apparently, if I didn't ask, he wasn't going to volunteer the information. "Are there any other messages from him in the book?"

"Yes," he said. "He starred certain chapters."

"What's in those chapters?"

Howard shrugged. "Well, I haven't read them all yet. I always read in order."

Of course. "Well, um . . . can I see what he marked? Real quick?"

Howard considered this. "Okay. But give it right back. I've just gotten to the chapter on 'Key Development and Authentication.'"

I nodded, and he handed over the book. As I checked out the table of contents, I noted that "Key Development and Authentication" was also starred. In fact, most of the starred chapters seemed to be about ciphers and keys. The stars fell off considerably after that, but I saw a few more toward the end, in the section entitled Applied Cryptology.

"What are 'Secret Broadcasts and Numbers Stations'?" I asked, reading.

He snatched back the book. "I'll let you know when I get to that part."

Nate looked over his shoulder and laughed. "No one tells my brother how to read a book."

I tried to look over at what Howard was reading, but he curled his arm protectively around the page and I gave up, sitting back and looking out the window as the green summer landscape flashed by. Okay. Howard read fast and he'd already broken one of the codes—I could wait until he figured out what Dr. Underberg was trying to tell us.

I hoped it was something good.

WE HAD TO unload the van when we arrived at the Guidant campus.

The guard at the gate explained. "No gas-powered vehicles are allowed on campus, but we have a fleet of electric cars that will take you to your destination." She waved us into a small parking garage whose roof was tiled with solar panels.

"They really like their green energy around here," Mom said as she parked. We grabbed our bags and walked back to the guard station.

"I'll need each of you to stand here," the guard said after she took our names. She pointed at an *X* on the floor in front of a large computer screen. "State your name into the camera, and then press your hand against this pad."

Eric grinned at the camera. "Eric Seagret." I saw the

screen behind his head flash with an image of his face, what looked like a green imprint of his palm, and the waveform of his voice.

We each took our turn giving our information to the machine.

"You're now ready to enter the campus," the guard said, as she pressed the surface of her tablet. "Your handprint will serve as your digital key for your housing, entrance to the amenities, equipment rental, and transportation passes. You can also use it for all transactions—if you're buying food, clothes, et cetera. Any questions?"

"Yeah," Eric said. "What do you do if you lose a hand?"

"Don't." The guard smiled. "Actually, if we have handicapped guests or employees, we issue a key card. Does that answer your question, young man?"

Eric said nothing.

"There are six of you, so you'll need two cars." She pointed, and we headed over to where the Guidant vehicles stood waiting for us. They looked like normal, small silver cars . . . at least from the outside.

"Um . . ." Nate looked into the driver's-side window. "Where's the steering wheel?"

We all took a closer peek. Inside the car, where there was usually a steering column and gas and brake pedals, stood nothing.

"Are they British?" Savannah asked, heading to the

other side. "Like we have to drive on the right?" She looked at the passenger seat, but there was no wheel on that side, either.

Nate climbed inside and pressed his hand against a panel where the steering column should have been.

"Welcome, Nate Noland," said a cheery woman's voice. "Please state your destination."

"Cool!" Eric exclaimed. "It's a self-driving car! Can I get in the driver's seat? Please-please-please?"

"Wait," my mother said. "They drive . . . by themselves?"

"Come on, Mom! Please?" Eric jumped up and down. He was clearly in heaven. All week long, he'd been gushing about the advanced technology at the Guidant campus, but I'd thought we'd just see stuff during our tour. I hadn't realized we'd be using their inventions ourselves. All weekend.

"If Nate doesn't mind," Mom said.

"Knock yourself out," said Nate, and climbed in the back. Eric hopped up front, and Howard took shotgun. It wasn't until Savannah climbed in next to Nate that I realized my error.

"Hey, guys?" Mom said. She was standing by the other car. "Who's riding with me?"

The others looked up at me from their seats. Uh-oh.

"Coming," I said flatly. So now all my friends were

going in one car, and I was stuck with Mom. I shuffled over to the other car to find her already seated on the passenger side.

"You can drive," she said with a sly smile.

I dumped my bag in the back and plopped down on the seat, pressing my hand against the panel.

"Gillian Seagret," the voice said, and even pronounced the G correctly. "Please state your destination."

Mom held up the directions Dad had emailed her.

"Forty-five Galileo Lane," I told the car. With a nearly inaudible hum, it started up, backed itself out of its parking space, and started off.

"This is pretty neat," Mom said, looking at the controls. "As long as I don't put my foot through the floorboard. I wonder how it knows to brake."

The car cruised along at a comfortable clip, not too fast and not too slow. Sometimes it decelerated at intersections as other cars came across the road, and sometimes it surged forward. "They must know where all the other cars are, all the time," I said.

"I've read about these before," Mom said, her grip on the door handle firm. "But I still can't imagine how it's safe."

I wanted to say, *Maybe that's because you're a history professor and not an automotive engineer.*

Or, *If you don't think it's safe, then what are we doing in one?*

Or, *Actually, what are you doing here at all? No one invited* you *to talk about Omega City.*

But I didn't say any of those things, because before I got a chance to, Mom spoke again.

"So what were you and Howard so engrossed in during the drive out here?"

"Oh, um, he was showing me how the codes in his book work." I wondered if, in the other car, Howard was telling Eric how the book really was from Dr. Underberg, who seemed to be alive and well after all. Too bad I'd miss seeing the look on his face.

"That sounds fun," Mom replied. "Did he ever figure out who the book came from?"

I looked down at my feet. Mom was right. It was weird to be sitting in a car with no steering column or gearbox. There was just so much space at our feet. "Actually, yes." I looked up at her. "It was from Dr. Underberg."

Mom's eyes widened. "Really? How do you know?"

"The inscription in the front was a code, and Howard broke it."

Mom's eyebrows furrowed. She looked so much like Eric when she did that. "But are you sure it was really him who wrote the coded message?"

"I already thought it was him," I said, "before Howard broke the code. I know his handwriting pretty well from helping Dad and then, last year, when we were in Omega City."

Mom took this in. "You should definitely tell your father. I know he'd love to speak to Dr. Underberg himself. He didn't seem to think there was a chance he survived in the rocket ship, but if he's gone into hiding again . . ." Mom shook her head. "This is all so incredible."

That wasn't the only thing that was incredible. "How do you know Dad doesn't think Dr. Underberg survived?"

She looked up at me, blinking in confusion. "I figured if your dad thought he was alive, he never would have published the book without interviewing him. But there's nothing from Underberg in the book."

Mom had read *The Forgotten Fortress*?

We'd started to pass buildings, shops, and houses. From what I'd read about the campus, I knew that the people who worked for Guidant brought their families to live here full-time. They did their shopping here, and the kids attended Guidant's state-of-the-art charter schools. The campus had gyms and sports centers and dance studios and hair salons and restaurants. It was like a little town, all built for the company and the people who lived and worked inside. I looked out the window to see the other car keeping pace with ours. Eric pressed his nose against the glass and made a face at us as their car sped by while ours slowed at the intersection.

"Hmm," Mom said, watching them weave through the cars. "I wonder if they have theirs on some kind of daredevil setting. I wouldn't put it past your brother."

"I didn't know you'd read Dad's book." I toed at the pristine beige carpet under my feet. I thought she hated everything Dad did.

"Of course I did," Mom said. "It stars my children." She reached her hand across the gulf between us. "And if and when he finishes the next one, I'll read that, too, though the Shepherds are my least favorite people on the planet."

Huh. I'd never thought of it like that. When the Shepherds had destroyed Dad's academic reputation, Mom's had gone in the toilet as well. When the Shepherds had pretended a pipe had burst so they could flood the cottage and ruin Dad's research . . . well, it had been Mom's cottage then, too. When the Shepherds scared Dad so bad he took us all off grid, Mom had suffered just as much as the rest of us.

"Though I don't know," she said now, staring off into the distance.

"Don't know what?" I pressed.

"I don't know if he's really going to write it."

"Of course he is!" I said. Dad wasn't going to back down just because it was hard to get people to talk to him about the Shepherds. Nothing had stopped him last time. Not losing his job, not losing *Mom* . . .

She shrugged. "It's none of my business. Not anymore—at least, not unless it puts you kids in danger. But I think it's strange. Someone came after your father for writing about Dr. Underberg. That we know. But now Sam—your dad—has published a whole book on Omega City, and no one has gone after him for it. It makes me wonder . . ." She cast me a sidelong glance. "Maybe the Shepherds didn't care about the discovery of Omega City. Maybe what they were afraid of him finding out was something else entirely."

I sat back in my seat, stunned. As much as I hated to admit it, Mom had a point. Whoever it was who'd destroyed my father's reputation after he wrote the Underberg book had been ruthless. Efficient. Relentless. But now that Dad supposedly knew who they were, shouldn't they be threatening us even more?

"Either way, I'll sleep better at night knowing we're under the same roof again."

I scowled.

"I know how hard last year was for you, Gillian. It was hard for me, too. That's why I think it's so important that we're all together in Idaho this fall. I've missed you and Eric so much. And your dad thinks it's only fair I get time with you, too."

Yeah, but then who would get time with Dad? Who would help him unmask the Shepherds, once and for all? My eyes started to sting, so I turned away and looked out the window again before I did anything as stupid as crying. Mom was the one who'd walked out. She couldn't just act like she deserved to walk right back in and pick up where she left off.

"Oh, sweetie . . ." Her hand ghosted against my hair, then vanished as the car slowed and I saw Dad standing in the driveway of the town house, waving wildly to us.

"You may now exit the vehicle," said the car, but I didn't need any prompting as I launched myself from my seat and catapulted into Dad's arms. I felt him squeezing me into a hug against his button-down, breathed in his familiar scent, and knew I was finally home.

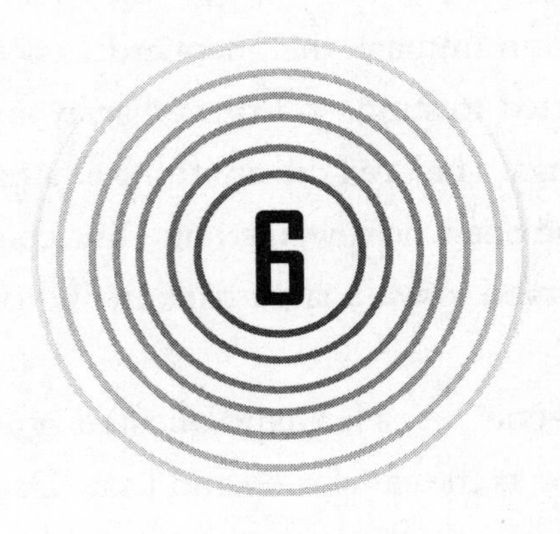

6

PLAY THE GAME

I'D THOUGHT WE'D BE STAYING IN HOTEL ROOMS, BUT THIS WAS MORE like a mansion. Dad called it a "visitor home," and it had three bedrooms, a living room, kitchen, dining room—and it all looked like a futuristic movie set. Every appliance was brand-new and brimming with crazy technology.

The refrigerator kept track of what you put in it and took out of it, and warned you if you were low on things like milk and eggs. The freezer could be set to defrost food if you told it to. The microwave, stove, and coffee machine had voice controls. And that was just the kitchen. When Savannah and I went into the bathroom, we realized that we could set the tub and sink faucets to dispense water at any temperature we wanted, just by saying so, and there was a motion-activated soap dispenser, like you sometimes saw in public bathrooms—except it held shampoo, conditioner, body wash, shaving cream, and moisturizer, too. There were fans and heat lamps, and some contraption that could dry, curl, or straighten hair, which Savannah said we had to try before our talk. We were still figuring out the settings when we heard a yelp from the boys' bathroom and Eric emerged, his face pale.

"What is it?" Savannah asked.

"The . . . toilet." Eric shook his head. "Don't go near the toilets."

"Why?" I was baffled.

Nate chuckled. "It tried to wash his butt."

Of course, since this was Guidant, all the rooms had tablets as well as those voice-activated thingies on the wall. We could set the temperature and lights any way we wanted, just by stating our preferences. The TVs in the bedrooms and living rooms all had personalized settings, too. Even the backyard was high-tech.

"Guidant is dedicated to green development and sustainability," Dad explained as we clustered around the back door. "All the homes have geothermal pumps and solar panels, to try to reduce the campus's reliance on fossil fuel energy."

"That's why the cars are all electric?" Nate asked.

"If they really wanted to save the planet," said Savannah, "wouldn't they make all their employees eat vegan?"

Eric rolled his eyes and pointed at the yard. "They don't look like they like plants much here."

I saw his point. There wasn't a single plant in the entire backyard—just a smooth surface made of gigantic, hexagonal plates of glass.

"Not entirely true," said Dad. "Guidant believes that normal grass lawns are a waste of water resources, so all the lawns are either artificial, so they don't require water, or natural green space with native plants. They don't do grass."

"Are those the solar panels?" Howard asked.

"Yes, but they're actually even more than that." Dad grinned. "It's called a smart court. I specially requested we get a visitor home that had one installed."

I looked at him, pretty sure this was more than he knew about our own house. "How do you know all this?"

He tapped the tablet by the door. "Research, Gillian. That's what I do. Come on, let's check it out."

Eric started toward the door, then paused. "Are you coming, Mom?"

I also cast a glance back at Mom, who was intently studying her phone screen. "No, no. You kids have fun with your dad."

We spilled onto the back patio, squinting a little as the

sunlight reflected up from the glass and the silver surface of Howard's Omega City utility suit.

Close up, I could see that the panels were made from a faceted greenish glass. At the edge of the patio was a small, waist-high pedestal with a panel, a speaker, and a screen set into the top. Next to the pedestal was a container filled with tennis balls, basketballs, soccer balls, rackets of all shapes and sizes, lacrosse and field hockey sticks, and baseball bats and gloves.

"No way," said Nate with a gasp. He put his hand on the pad.

"Hello, Nate Noland," came a voice from the speaker. "Would you like to play a game?" Dad, standing behind us, laughed as the screen flickered to life with a dozen options.

"I don't get it," I said. "Is it a giant video game?"

"Yes!" Eric hissed in glee.

"No," said Nate. He pressed a button and the panels came alive. White lines glowed up from the panes, rectangles and circles materializing on the surface as if a giant hand was painting a basketball court in front of our eyes.

"Check it out!" Eric cried, scrolling through the screen. "You can do batting practice or tennis or half-court basketball or soccer . . . wait, how do they do the nets and goals and stuff?"

As if in response, a little door opened at either end of the court and poles telescoped out of the ground, rising to regulation height as a backboard and hoop fanned out from the top, a bit like an automated umbrella.

Nate grabbed a ball and headed down the steps to the court, and Savannah ran after him. "I'll play if I can be on Nate's team."

"No fair!" Eric called down at her. "I want to be on Nate's team. Girls versus boys."

"Like that solves anything?" Savannah said. "We don't have even numbers of girls and boys."

I looked at the court display on the screen in front of us. Along with the outline of the basketball court, it showed Savannah's and Nate's position as little dots. So it could even see where we stood? Though I supposed that made sense, especially if it wanted to see if we were inbounds or offsides.

Although how could it tell what team we were on?

"Nate has nine inches on me," Savannah whined.

"And I'm shorter than you are," Eric pointed out.

"And he sucks at basketball, either way," Howard said. He was still standing next to the screen, scrolling through the court choices. "We should try four square." He pressed his finger against the screen and the basketball poles snapped shut and began retracting as the lines on the panels began to fade and get redrawn like a giant Etch A Sketch.

"Quit it!" Nate cried up at his brother, who ignored him.

"The problem," Howard went on as he pressed the screen again, making the lines on the court disintegrate and re-form, "is that there's really no way for the court to pretend to be a grass field. You might be able to play basketball or tennis, but not soccer or any other field sports."

"Knock it off!" Nate yelled up at him. "We want to play!" He leaped out of the way as a crack opened in the center of the court and a wire tennis net began to unfold. Nate stormed up the stairs. "I said *stop*!"

"Um . . ." Howard jammed his fingers against the screen. "I think I overloaded it." The lines kept erasing and redrawing, as doors snapped open and shut, with whirring goals and poles and baskets and nets unfurling and retracting at once.

"You broke it?" Savannah rolled her eyes. "Again with the buttons, Howard?"

Nate lunged at Howard, who sidestepped him and jumped off the porch onto the court. Nate chased after him while I tried to figure out how he'd broken the controls. Buttons were not Howard's strong suit.

Howard ducked under a retreating basketball hoop and hopped over the sinking tennis net, with his brother hot on his heels. I tried to wrangle the touch screen. "Help me," I said to my brother. "Poke anything that looks like an escape button."

"Ah," Eric said from behind me. "This brings me back to that elevator where we were almost gassed to death." He leaned over my shoulder. "That's weird," he said, and pointed at where the dot of Nate was circling the court and trying to pin down his brother down.

"What?" I asked.

"Howard's invisible." He tapped the screen where we should have seen a dot for Howard, but the screen was dark.

"No wonder Guidant's not selling these things yet," I said. "They still need to work out the bugs."

Nate tackled Howard to the ground.

"Lemme up!" Howard shouted, scrabbling with hands and feet to try to get leverage on the smooth surface.

"Stop messing around," Nate shot back, and sat on top of him. Howard pushed up and kicked his legs out like a donkey to unseat Nate. On the screen, another person-dot flickered to life underneath Nate's.

I narrowed my eyes and peered closer. Eric was right. The court only recognized him when his hands were on the ground, not when any part of the utility suit was.

"Okay, guys," said Dad. "That's enough. I don't think the smart court has a wrestling option. Plus, it doesn't have, um, cushioned mats."

But that didn't stop them.

THE INCIDENT WITH the smart court left Howard with a scraped knee and Nate with a bruise the size of a quarter on his upper arm.

"Ow, dude," Nate said to his brother as they sat around the guesthouse kitchen, icing their wounds and eating lunch. "When did you get so strong?"

"Why did it take you so long to notice?" Howard shot back.

Savannah shook her head at the two of them. "I should probably be glad I'm an only child, huh?"

"Yes," Eric and I said in unison.

Dad laughed and ruffled my brother's hair. "I missed you guys."

I hugged him from behind. "We missed you, too."

Mom was in the other room, "giving us space" or whatever, while she answered some work emails. I wished she'd either just dropped us off and left us alone, or stayed to see what it was she was trying to wreck with her whole Idaho plan. We belonged with Dad.

She poked her head in and tapped the face of her watch. "Are you guys going to be ready? We have our tour soon."

That reminded me. "Dad, yesterday was Howard's birthday—"

"Oh, really? Happy birthday, Howard," Dad said absentmindedly. He was standing at the kitchen counter, shuffling papers into a file.

"And he got a book on code breaking," I continued.

"That's great. Codes are fun." He frowned at one of his printouts, then shoved it in an envelope.

"We think it's from Dr. Underberg."

Finally, Dad turned his attention to me. "What?"

"It's true, Dr. S.," Howard said. "It's got an inscription inside that says it's from him."

Dad narrowed his eyes. "And someone sent that to you? That just seems cruel. . . ."

I blinked. Cruel? Did that mean Dad thought it was impossible, too? "It was in his handwriting, Dad!" I exclaimed. "The code, I mean. Howard, go get the book."

"You recognize his handwriting?" Dad asked as Howard ran to retrieve it.

"Of course," I exclaimed. "I recognized it last year, in the stolen diary pages I found on, um, Fiona's computer."

Dad was looking at me sadly. "Right. My daughter, the sneak."

"The sneak who found out what that woman was up to," Mom pointed out. "And she *is* your daughter, Sam. You would have done the exact same thing."

"Good point," Dad conceded.

I looked at Mom. Who would have thought she'd stand up for me? About snooping. To *Dad.* Was today opposite day?

Howard came back with the code book and handed it to Dad, who flipped to the inscription. "This does look like Underberg's writing. . . ."

I smirked at Eric, but when I turned back to Dad, his face was drawn with concern.

"I don't like this."

"I do," said Howard, reaching out as if Dad was going to take the book away. "It has a lot of information on substitution ciphers and letter frequency and numbers stations."

Dad gave him a weak smile. "That's not what I mean, Howard. I just think it's odd that you would get a book like this, that claims to be from Underberg, when we haven't heard anything about him in months."

"It is from him!" I insisted. "I'd know that handwriting anywhere."

Dad handed the book back to Howard, who looked relieved. "Then isn't it possible other people recognize his handwriting, too? And if they were trying to convince you a message came from Dr. Underberg, using his handwriting would be exactly the way they'd do it?"

I leaned back in my seat. He had a point there.

"I can understand how strongly you want to believe Dr. Underberg is still out there, honey," Dad was saying now. "I want to believe it, too. The idea of meeting the man I've devoted so much of my life to researching—it would be a dream come true. But I've tried to find him, over and over. Ever since you guys escaped from Omega City, I've been searching—calling all my old sources, contacting my friends in the aeronautics industry, both before the book was published and since, to get a definitive answer on what happened to him and his rocket. But no one knows anything. At least, not anything they would tell me."

Before *The Forgotten Fortress* was published and Dad's reputation was redeemed, this wouldn't have surprised me. But after?

"And then this package arrives for Howard. It seems . . . strange, to say the least."

"What do you mean?" Nate asked.

"Someone sent this to Howard—not to me, who has been trying to get in contact with Underberg for months."

"And not to me," Eric said. "I had a birthday, too, you know."

"And whoever did it had to know what a message from Dr. Underberg would mean to you kids."

His words hung in the air for a second as we pondered what this meant. Savannah gasped.

"Ooh," she cried. "Do you mean—could it be from Fiona, Dr. S.?"

I felt cold. I'd never thought about that. Eric and I didn't know if Fiona and her assistants had ended up facing jail time for the stuff they did to us, but I do know Dad took out a restraining order against all three of them.

Maybe that's why the book was sent to Howard, instead of to either of us.

Fiona was part of the team of Shepherds who'd destroyed Dad's reputation by flooding our cottage and all his research documents, making him unable to prove his sources when doubt was cast on his work. She'd stolen Dr. Underberg's personal diary from my dad so she could find Omega City and claim all of Underberg's inventions for herself. She'd pretended to date Dad so she could weasel even more information about Underberg out of him. She'd chased me and my friends all through the city and tried to trap us inside. She'd blown up Omega City and forced Dr. Underberg into space. I hated her.

And I'd hate her even more if she made us think Dr. Underberg was still alive when he wasn't.

ET IN ARCADIA, EGO

DAD RECOMMENDED WE PAUSE OUR CONVERSATION AND GET DRESSED IN our nice clothes for the meeting with the Guidant engineers, and we agreed. The book wasn't going anywhere.

In the car on the way over, Eric slid in beside me.

"Hey," he said.

"Hey," I replied.

"Truce?"

I frowned. So now that Dad agreed there was something to worry about, Eric believed me? Good to know.

"Come on, Gills," he coaxed. "I thought you were just trying to come up with another reason not to go to Idaho. . . ."

"Well, I'm not!" I snapped.

"I know that now." He looked at his hands. "I'm sorry, okay? The next time you tell me something completely bonkers, I promise not to question it."

I stared at him. "There's no way you're going to pull that off."

He shrugged, and a smile sneaked back onto his face. "I just said the *next* time. Not every time. As a favor."

I considered this as Guidant buildings flashed by outside the window. "Okay," I said at last. "Truce."

All the structures on the Guidant campus were designed to be as environmentally friendly as possible, which meant many were covered in solar panels or had moss-covered roofs that supposedly cleaned water and offset pollution. The building where the cars stopped featured a soaring glass atrium filled with a landscape of trees, bushes, and fountains.

As soon as we were inside, a young woman walked briskly up to us. "Hello!" she said brightly. "I'm Dani Alcestis, Elana Mero's assistant. We're so happy to have you here."

Dani was a tall, pretty, young woman with green eyes, light brown skin, and straightened hair that had been sculpted into a big bronze swirl at the crown of her head. She smoothed a hand across her hair as she spoke. "Unfortunately, I have some bad news. Ms. Mero was called away at the last moment and will be unable to meet with you as planned this afternoon. But she's looking forward to seeing you tonight. We've arranged for a dinner at one of the campus's best restaurants."

"Oh," said Dad. He looked at Mom and Nate. "We weren't all planning on staying. Nate has a college tour he's supposed to go to."

Dani's eyes flicked in Nate's direction. "You're leaving? I don't think Ms. Mero was aware you wouldn't all be staying for the whole weekend."

"I hope that's not a problem," Dad said.

Dani hesitated for a moment, then smiled politely. "No, not at all. It's just unfortunate that she won't get the chance to meet him. Ms. Mero was so taken with your stories in *The Forgotten Fortress*. She was looking forward to a chance to meet personally with each of you." She straightened her jacket. "I've read the book, too, and I was very impressed, especially with your account of actually speaking to Dr. Underberg. What an honor, to be able to converse with such a brilliant man."

"Well," I said, "maybe he'll come back to Earth one day, and you can talk to him, too."

Dani gave me a curious glance. "You must be Gillian."

I nodded.

"I think it would be an amazing experience, to get to talk to Dr. Underberg, as you did." She looked thoughtful.

"Unlike you, I may even have taken him up on his offer to go to the stars."

I looked at her in surprise. Really? Even though no one knew what happened to his ship? Most everyone else who'd read Dad's book thought Underberg was crazy for taking off like that—and even crazier for trying to coax a bunch of kids to join him.

"So who are we meeting with?" Howard asked.

Dani blinked, as if lost in thought, and straightened. "The engineers, of course. Everyone here has read your book and is excited to discuss your discoveries. And of course, we want to show you all the behind-the-scenes developments here at Eureka Cove and give you an idea about the ways we hope to bring Underberg's dreams to life in the twenty-first century."

"Cool," said Howard. "Hey, I read that Guidant is interested in starting a space flight program, like SpaceX."

"Yes," Dani said. "It's a lot different from when I was a kid, and the only space exploration in the country was being done by NASA. But Guidant is still several years away from launching any manned flights. Our only real triumph in that field is with our satellite, Capella."

"That's the early-warning satellite that detected that comet last week?" Howard asked.

"We're still monitoring it," Dani said.

"I heard about that," said Mom. "They said it will pass

almost as close to Earth as the moon."

"That's a little too close, isn't it?" Nate asked. "I mean, can't it hit us?"

"It's less than two thousand feet wide, and it's about three hundred thousand miles away," said Howard. "So, no." He thought for a second, then added, "Well, hopefully, no."

"Hopefully?" Nate's eyes widened.

"The Capella project monitors all near-Earth objects that pose a threat to our planet," Dani said. "Though here at Guidant we're focused on making the Earth as beautiful and sustainable a place as possible. You know what they say: *Et in Arcadia, ego.*"

"What?" I narrowed my eyes. "What about Arkadia?"

Dad chuckled. "It's Latin, Gillian. A famous Latin saying. *Et in Arcadia, ego.* Arcadia was a term for a classical natural paradise."

"Is that what Arkadia Group was named for?" Savannah asked.

"Oh, that's right," exclaimed Dani. "Arkadia Group, like in your book, Dr. Seagret."

"But what does it mean?" I asked. "*Et in Arcadia* . . . whatever . . ."

"'Even in Arcadia, I am,'" Mom broke in. "Except the 'I' is death."

"Death?" Nate echoed.

"Yes," Mom said. "The saying means that no matter how perfect things appear, death still awaits."

"Wicked," said Eric.

"Gross," said Savannah.

"Huh," said Dani, turning to my father. "You know, Dr. Seagret, it's interesting, what Gillian here said. Maybe this Arkadia Group Dr. Underberg was a part of did take their name from the saying. After all, they were the people who helped Underberg build Omega City, right? Preparing for the end of the world, even at the height of the twentieth century?"

"Good point," said Dad. "At the very least, I think we've found a chapter title for the new book."

"Excellent." Dani clapped her hands. "Now, shall we start the tour?"

As everyone trotted off behind Dani, I took one last look around the atrium. The soaring, glass panes, the gurgling fountains, the carefully manicured trees . . .

Et in Arcadia, ego.

I HAD TO admit it—the Guidant facilities were amazing. I was sure even Dr. Underberg would agree. I wondered if he'd be working for a company like this now, if he hadn't disappeared into Omega City all those decades ago. If he'd be getting involved in all these private companies' space exploration programs. What wonderful things could he have invented if Arkadia Group hadn't turned on him and driven him—literally—underground? Self-driving cars, robotic limbs, computers you could control with your eyes—and that was just the stuff I could understand!

Maybe Eric was right, and Guidant *was* the way to help Dr. Underberg's battery reach the masses.

The first place Dani took us was the Guidant Renewable Energy Lab, where they showed us prototypes for cell phones that could charge in the sun on the dashboard of a car.

"Wow," said Dad. "Totally renewable energy would be even better than the Underberg battery."

"Or," said one of the engineers, "we could combine the technologies to create a battery that would charge easily and last for a long time."

I looked at Dad, but he didn't even seem fazed by the statement. Then again, I didn't know what kind of conversations he might have already had with Guidant. Maybe he was going to give them the prototype to the battery, and just . . . hadn't gotten around to mentioning it to us yet.

I supposed I couldn't expect him to tell us everything that had happened on his book tour. I should probably get used to it, too. After all, if we were off in Idaho, we'd have no idea what was going on with him.

After the scientists finished showing us their work, they started asking questions about Omega City. I was surprised to see how many of them had copies of *The Forgotten Fortress* at their desks.

"How many machines did you see in the city that were powered by battery?" one of the engineers asked.

"Well," said Nate, "not very many of the machines worked, so . . ."

"The flashlights were," Howard answered. "And I'm still trying to figure out what's powering the suits. . . ."

The engineers crowded around him and began examining the utility suit. "It's not solar?" said one. Another tugged on the sleeve panels while a third unzipped one of the cargo pockets. When a fourth began patting him down, looking for battery packs in the kneepads, Howard yelped and skittered away.

"Why don't you leave it here?" an engineer asked.

"No!" said Howard, covering the zipper pulls protectively.

"Don't worry," said Dani. "We'd never make you give up your utility suit. Sorry, ladies and gentlemen. Howard doesn't have anything else to wear."

"They can have mine," Savannah whispered beside me.

Howard rejoined us. "They broke the zipper pull," he whined. The hexagonal piece of metal glittered in his palm.

"Looks like they just disconnected it," said Savannah.

"No," Howard insisted. "They broke it. Look." He pinched the metal between his fingers, and it folded like origami.

"Hmm." Savannah frowned. "We'll fix it later. Here, I'll hold it for you."

Howard glumly handed it over, and Savannah put it in her purse. I chose not to tell her how often I'd seen Howard sucking on it. If you asked me, that was the real reason it broke off.

The engineers were just as excited to see us in every department we visited. In the Agricultural Tech Lab, they quizzed us about what we'd seen in the Omega City greenhouse (mostly dead plants), and in the Transportation Research Department, we talked for twenty minutes about elevators.

"Were you afraid in the elevator shaft?" one computer engineer asked me as he gave me his copy of *The Forgotten Fortress* to sign.

"Yes," I said, feeling a little embarrassed. "I was afraid the whole time. But I didn't really think about it. I just thought about getting out."

"That's really amazing focus for a girl your age," he said.

Was that a compliment? I wasn't sure. "Thank you?" I was relieved when he moved on.

"Show me where you broke your teeth," another employee asked Eric, who promptly gave him a wide grin.

"Wow, you can't even tell!"

Everywhere we went, the employees had read Dad's book and were full of questions. Dad hung back for the most part, letting us tell them about our experiences in the city firsthand. In the Jet Lab, everyone wanted to know technical specs for the rocket ship, but not even Howard had much to tell them about that. Eventually, Dani had to cut the engineers off.

"If only you'd gotten a closer look at the tiles lining the silo," one scientist remarked sadly.

"Sorry, dude," said Nate. "We were too busy running for our lives."

At the end, we visited the department working on the Capella project, the giant satellite telescope Guidant had built to help NASA and other space organizations take pictures of NEOs, or "near-Earth objects." The scientists working on Capella would analyze the data of all the asteroids and comets and other space debris that looked like they had a chance of hitting the Earth.

"It's basically like meteorology . . . for actual meteors," Dani explained. "The further in advance we can identify possible dangers, the more likely we are to be able to divert them or otherwise make sure that they don't cause problems down here on Earth."

"Like the asteroid that killed the dinosaurs?" Howard asked.

"That would definitely be a worst-case scenario," Dani said. "An extinction-level event."

"What's an extinction-level event?" Savannah looked horrified.

"Exactly what it sounds like," said Nate. "A thing that makes us extinct."

Savannah squeaked.

Dani nodded seriously. "We're looking out for those, too. But we're also hoping to avoid smaller but still dangerous asteroids. It doesn't have to be big to do a lot of damage. Even a small collision could cause tidal waves or airbursts that could destroy electronics systems. Have any of you heard of the Tunguska event? It was what astronomers call an airburst, a meteor strike where the meteor burned up before impact, but the shock wave flattened everything for miles all around."

Howard turned to me. "See?" he said. "Tunguska *was* a meteor."

I rolled my eyes. *Sure* it was.

"Why is it called Capella?" Howard asked.

"One of the reasons is that Capella is one of the brightest stars in the sky," Dani replied. "Elana thought it was fitting with Guidant, you know . . . *leading the way* and all that."

"*One* of the reasons?" I asked. "Are there others?"

"Capella is the Goat Star," Howard interrupted. "I don't

usually think of goats as leaders."

"No," said Nate with a grin, "more like stubborn loners, right, Howard?"

Dani's smile was more strained. "But stubborn loners can get the job done, right? Like Dr. Underberg. Or your father."

I had to admit, the Capella lab was cool, a large, dark room with huge screens on all the walls showing images of space rocks glittering like massive, fiery jewels, and possible trajectory paths glowing like necklaces across the solar system.

"Pretty!" Savannah exclaimed.

"Isn't it?" said Dani. "Ms. Mero designed the lab herself. It always makes me think of that song 'Lucy in the Sky with Diamonds.'"

"Never heard of it," said Savannah. "What about 'Twinkle, Twinkle, Little Star'?"

Dani laughed. "Okay, that one works, too."

"It makes me feel safe," Mom said, staring in wonder at the pictures. "Knowing that someone is watching the skies."

"Unfortunately," said Dani, "we're a lot better at seeing things coming than being able to stop them."

I shivered. All of a sudden the dark, cavernous space reminded me more of Omega City, a desperate attempt by humans to save ourselves from forces far, far beyond our control.

I was relieved when we returned to the sunny atrium. Near the front doors, Dani stopped, turned to us, and said, "Now, you still have about three or four hours before your dinner to explore the campus and have a little fun. There's smart-court bowling and minigolf, or you could check out our drones, or go boating on the cove . . ."

"You kids go ahead," Dad said. "I've got a few emails I have to return to help plan the fall tour schedule."

I didn't like the sound of that. This was our first chance to hang out with Dad in weeks and he was going to work the whole time?

"And you, Nate," Dani said. "Enjoy your college visit. Where are you going again?"

As Dani and Nate started talking about college admissions, I tugged Dad's sleeve. "You aren't going to come with us today?" At the very least, I wanted to talk to him about Howard's book and what it might mean for finding Dr. Underberg.

He shook his head. "I really have to get back to work. But don't worry. We'll have all day tomorrow to hang out, okay?"

We said our good-byes to Nate, and to Mom, who was switching cars with Dad and heading back home. "It was so much fun hearing your stories today," she told Eric, ruffling his hair. "I'm really proud of you. But I have to be honest, I don't know if I'll ever be able to listen to your story without having a panic attack."

"Mo-om." Eric shoved her hand away.

"Just promise me no more death-defying adventures, okay? Or at least call me first?"

"Don't worry, Dr. S.," said Savannah. "I'm never going off exploring again."

Mom held out her arms for me. "Hug before I go?"

I dutifully trotted over.

"You were so amazing today, sweetie," she said softly. "You're becoming such an impressive young woman, and it was a privilege to listen to you tell your story."

"Thank you," I mumbled into her shirt.

"All right," she said, and pulled away. "I'll see you guys at home. Have a great weekend!"

She waved and headed off with Nate, while we went with Dad and Dani back to the town house to change into playclothes and swimsuits.

When we were ready, Dani met us at the front door. "You guys going to be okay on your own?"

We all looked at her, bewildered.

"We managed Omega City," Eric said. "I think we can handle Eureka Cove."

She raised her hands. "You have me there. Okay, you know how to work the cars. Remember, don't leave any items in a vehicle when you leave, because it goes to where it's called. If you need to call a new one, just look for the blue boxes on the light posts—they all have call buttons. A car will come pick you up. They come equipped with maps and phone directories. If you have any problems, you can use the box to call me or your dad and we'll come get you. Remember, you can always buy food or rent equipment using your handprint."

The four of us climbed into the car.

"Where to?" Savannah asked. "Should we give the smart courts another try?"

"No," Eric said. "Let's get on the water. I want to see what kind of high-tech boats they have."

My brother and his one-track mind. "But you're the only one who can sail."

"Okay, then let's take out a motorboat," Eric said. "Think those are self-driving, too?"

"Yeah," Savannah agreed. "We could go tubing or something. It's so nice and warm out, we should check out the cove."

Howard pressed his hand against the panel.

"Howard Noland," said the car. "Please state your destination."

"Please take us to Eureka Cove," he replied.

The car didn't move. "We are currently located at Guidant Technologies Eureka Cove Campus. Please state your destination."

We all looked at one another, helpless.

After a minute, the car spoke again. "Would you like a list of popular destinations on the campus?"

"Take us to the boats," Eric tried.

Nothing happened.

"I don't think you're an authorized user," Savannah said, gesturing to Howard.

"Please take us to the boats?" Howard tried.

"Would you like to travel to the docks and boat rentals on the Eureka Cove beach?" the car asked.

"Yes!" we all exclaimed.

The car, thankfully, responded by starting off.

"I don't really care what we do," Howard said as we drove along, "as long as I can keep reading my book. I'm reading a chapter about radio stations they use to send spy messages and how difficult they are to decode."

"Radio presets on," said the car, and a weather report began to play through the speaker. "Please choose a station."

"Ooh, make it play music!" Savannah said.

"I don't want to listen to music," said Howard. "I want to read the chapter on the numbers stations."

The radio went static for a moment, and I watched the numbers on the digital preset roam up and down through the FM and then AM options, until they finally landed somewhere in the high thousands. A flat, computerized female voice began to speak.

"Seventeen, thirty-five, fifteen, twenty-two, forty-one, fifteen, twelve . . ."

Howard sat up straight in his seat. "It's a numbers station!"

The list of numbers went on like that for quite a while, and then stopped, replaced by these words:

Twinkle, twinkle, little star,
How I wonder what you are.
Up above the world so high
Like a diamond in the sky.

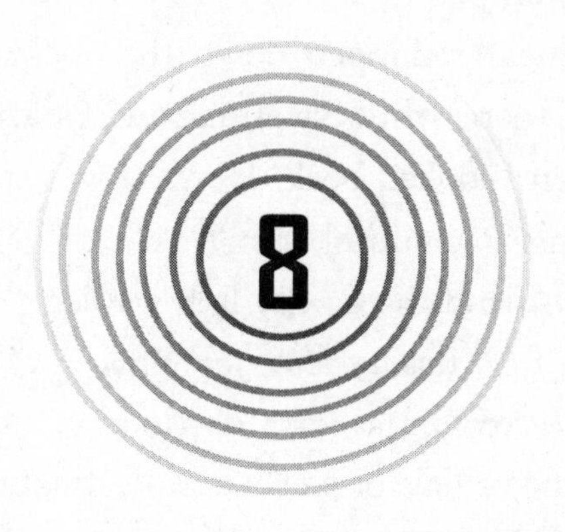

NURSERY RHYMES AND NANOTECH

"CREEPY," SAID SAVANNAH.

My mouth dropped open. Creepy . . . and suspicious. "Weren't we *just* talking about this song?"

Howard whipped out his pad of paper and was scribbling furiously as the woman started reciting numbers again.

"That's it," Savannah said. "I'm definitely controlling the car next time."

"*Fifteen, forty-two, twenty-three, thirty-four, fourteen, fifty-one, fifteen . . .*"

For a moment, the sound cut off, and the car said, "Arriving at Eureka Cove Beach, boat and equipment rental."

Howard slumped in his seat. "I missed the rest."

Eric practically skipped down the docks toward the boats moored there, while Savannah and I started to follow him, but when I looked back, Howard was still sitting in the car, writing down numbers.

"*Fourteen*," said the creepy lady's voice. "*Twenty-one, thirteen, fifty-five, twenty-four, forty-two* . . ."

"You have arrived at your destination," the car said. "Please exit the vehicle or pick a new destination."

"Shut up!" Howard snapped at the car. "I'm trying to listen."

I glanced at the others. Eric had already chosen a boat and had pressed his hand to the panel on the engine. He beckoned wildly to us.

I walked back and stood by the open door. "Come on, Howard. We're supposed to stick together."

"I want to get this down," he said, head bent low over his paper. "I don't care about tubing."

The woman on the radio kept saying numbers for another minute, and then:

Hey, diddle, diddle, the cat and the fiddle,
The cow jumped over the moon.
The little dog laughed to see such sport,
And the dish ran away with the spoon.

After that, the station went silent.

"Come on, Gills!" Eric called.

Okay, that was weird. We waited another minute, but nothing more came through.

"See?" I said to Howard. "The broadcast is over. Let's go. We can listen again another time."

Reluctantly, Howard climbed out of the car, his book and notebook firmly clutched in his hands. As soon as the door closed behind him, the car zipped off, as if it had already been summoned to another location.

"Do you think the boat has a radio?" Howard asked glumly as we headed down the dock.

Savannah and Eric had already loaded up an inflatable tube and the necessary lines, and were strapping on their life jackets as we climbed aboard.

"Life jackets, everyone," Eric said as the boat instructed him to double-check the lines before engaging the motor.

"Aye, aye, Captain." I gave him a mock salute and strapped in. Howard bent over his notebook again as we pulled away from the docks. The summer sun beat down from a cloudless sky, turning the rippling water into a cascade of sparkles. The beach was a golden stretch of sand dotted with cabanas and umbrellas, and we could see families and kids playing in the surf. On a day like today, it was impossible to imagine that, far up in space, hurtling toward us on a fiery path, might be a giant rock that spelled out the destruction of all mankind.

But I guess it was like Dani said: *Et in Arcadia, ego.*

"Eureka Cove is a man-made lagoon partially formed from what used to be polluted wetlands," the boat explained as we motored away from shore. "After Guidant Technologies bought this parcel of land, they engaged in a massive undertaking of environmental cleanup and reclamation. Now the Cove is a model of green engineering, and the adjoining wetlands is home to over two dozen threatened or endangered species."

"That's so awesome," Savannah said.

"As elsewhere on Guidant Technologies' Eureka Cove Campus, the cove is off-limits to gas-powered vehicles. This boat is fitted with a solar-powered battery and electric backup. It will automatically monitor battery levels and alert passengers when it is time to return to a charging station."

"I love the future." Eric grinned. "Okay, who's first in the tube?"

"Gillian and me!" Savannah cried. She'd already stripped down to her bathing suit and was clipping her life jacket back on. "Come on, let's go!"

I pulled off my shorts and left my sandals in the bottom of the boat. "Are you sure you're okay driving alone?" I asked my brother.

"What do you mean, *driving*?" Eric replied. "Boat, we'd like to go tubing."

"Please utilize location clips on passengers' life preservers," said the boat. "The motor will automatically cut off if passengers are thrown from the tube. Speed overrides in place. Enter the water when ready."

The boat slowed to an idle, and we tossed the inflatable tube overboard. On top of the tube were a pair of magnetic monitors that attached by a cord to little clips. Those must be the location clips. Savannah and I hopped on the tube and attached the clips to our jackets. There was enough slack that we could still bounce around on the tube without pulling the magnets free, but if we fell off, we'd take them with us.

"This is so cool," Eric called as the tube floated a little way away. "There's even a monitor here for the tension on the line. I don't need to do anything."

"Activating voice control for engine speed," I heard the boat say.

"Well," he corrected, "*hardly* anything."

Once the line was taut, Savannah gave the signal and the boat took off. We squealed and clung to the tube, laughing our heads off at every bounce and kick from the wake. Our path took us on a wide arc through the cove, so we could see the buildings of the Guidant campus flash by on the left-hand shore. To the right was a large, heavily wooded island, and as we got closer I could see a few buildings shrouded among the trees, as well as a rocky outcropping with what looked like a radio tower on top.

"This is awesome!" Savannah yelled in my ear. She held up her thumb to Eric. "Faster!"

The boat sped up, then began to swing us around to the right, when suddenly, the motor cut off. Momentum swished the tube closer to the boat, and we bobbed up and down on the waves created by the wake.

"What happened?" Savannah called to the boys. "We're not out of power already, are we?"

Eric was peering at the screen. "It says something about proximity limits."

I paddled over to the boat and hauled myself aboard. "Maybe it's saying we're too far off to return before the battery runs out?" I peered over his shoulder as he tapped the screen. "Oh, that's weird."

"What?"

"Well, all the buildings on the campus are marked on this map," I said, pointing out the labels on the digital map on the screen. Our boat was a blinking red dot in the blue lagoon. To the left were all the streets and landmarks of the campus. "But nothing's marked for the island."

"Maybe nothing's on it," Eric said. He banged his fist against the side of the control column. "Start, you stupid thing."

"No, there are buildings!" I said, and pointed at the island, but whatever I'd seen before was now hidden by trees. You could still catch sight of the radio tower on the outcropping, though.

"Proximity limit reached," the boat said. "Please specify destination."

"We're not going to a destination," Eric said to the boat. "We're going tubing."

"Proximity limit reached," the boat repeated. "Alternate route required."

"Is that all?" Eric asked. "Fine then, just turn to port."

"Location clip disengaged," the boat said. "Please reattach to continue."

"Here," I said, undoing my clip. "You take a turn. I don't like watching you argue with an inanimate object."

"Fine," Eric said, snapping the clip to his life jacket and jumping off the side. I pressed my hand to the boat's sensor panel.

"Welcome, Gillian Seagret," said the boat. "Proximity limit reached. Alternate route required."

"Okay," I said. "Keep going back in the direction of the docks."

The boat made a sharp turn to the left and motored slowly away from where Eric and Savannah bobbed on top of the tube. Once the line was taut, the boat said, "Activating voice control for engine speed."

I checked on Eric and Savannah, who gave me a thumbs-up.

"Faster," I told the boat, and it complied. I set us on a weaving pattern, so the tube could bop along back and forth over the wake, and smiled when Savannah and Eric screamed in delight. Howard was paying us no attention, crouched low over his notebook, his arm protecting the pages from sea spray.

"What are you doing?" I shouted to him.

"Trying to break the code, of course. But I'm not getting very far."

"Give yourself a break," I said. "You only got that book last night. Real code breakers use, like, computers and things to decrypt stuff."

"I didn't get enough of a sample to use letter frequency," he said. "Plus, there's no reason to think that the code is even a substitution cipher."

I assumed that was all code-breaking talk he'd picked up from his book. "Maybe it's not even a code," I said. "It was just random numbers and nursery rhymes."

"Faster!" Eric called from the tube.

"Faster," I said to the boat, which responded immediately.

"But that's how numbers stations work," Howard explained. "At least, according to the chapter Dr. Underberg starred in the book."

Maybe Dr. Underberg. But I didn't say that to Howard.

"They mix up their codes with songs or other messages that contain the keywords, and only the people receiving the transmission are supposed to know how to decode it."

"So you think that radio station we heard was a numbers station?" I shouted over the engine.

As the boat neared shore again, it made another wide turn to head back into the lagoon, and Eric and Savannah bounced over the wake behind us.

"Are you trying to kill us, Gills?" he screamed.

"Blame this screwy boat!" I called back, then turned to Howard.

"It played numbers, didn't it?" Howard asked. "Have you ever heard a radio station like that before?"

"If someone's actually broadcasting code from a radio station in Eureka Cove, don't you think the encryption would be too advanced to be broken by a twelve-year-old with his first code book?" I grabbed onto the rails as the boat veered right again. "Guidant is a tech firm. Encryption is what they *do*."

"Dr. Underberg sent me this book with the chapters marked, and then the very next day we hear a numbers station." He looked at me. "I don't think that's a coincidence."

He was right, but it still didn't make any sense. We didn't know if Dr. Underberg was even alive yesterday. What kind of code could he want us to break? How did he even know we'd be coming to Eureka Cove?

"What if you'd had your birthday party after we came back from Guidant? What if we'd left a day early and you'd waited until after you got back to open it?"

"I don't," Howard said. "I always open my birthday presents on my birthday."

"Well, what if you'd waited to start reading the book? You didn't read that book Nate got you yet."

Howard thought about this for a second. "I guess that's true."

Again, the boat engine cut off and I glanced up, sure I'd see that either Eric or Savannah had fallen off the tube.

"Proximity limit reached," the boat said. We bobbed up and down on the surface of the lagoon. The prow of the boat now faced the dark island. "Please specify alternate location."

"What is with this thing?" I asked, tapping the screen. "Why does it keep steering us to the limit?"

I checked behind us to see Eric and Savannah waving and gesturing to me. "Just a second!" I said. Behind them I could see the docks and the beach, not so far away. Not nearly as far as it had been when I had been out on the tube and we'd traveled up the shore.

"Boat," I said carefully. "Redirect us to go parallel to the shore."

The motor started up again, and the boat veered left.

"Voice control activated."

I checked on Eric and Savannah, then ordered the boat to speed up when they gave me the signal. As we sped away from the docks and up the coast, I ordered the boat to go faster and faster, to weave back and forth in the water so it got closer to the campus shore and then farther away, but I was always careful to keep a far distance from the island.

"Hey, Gillian," Howard said. "Can you see if the boat's radio gets reception for the numbers station, please? Eric wouldn't let me."

"You asked Eric?"

"Yeah," he said. "We were arguing about it right before you came onboard."

He meant right before the boat stopped. And earlier, in the car, when Howard said the words "numbers stations," the car went and found one for him on the radio.

"Radio station," I said out loud, to test my theory. The boat veered right, then promptly slowed.

"Proximity limit reached."

I looked ahead of us, at the radio tower winking through the island trees. It might not be marked on the map, but there was a radio station on that island.

And, as the boat said, it was off-limits.

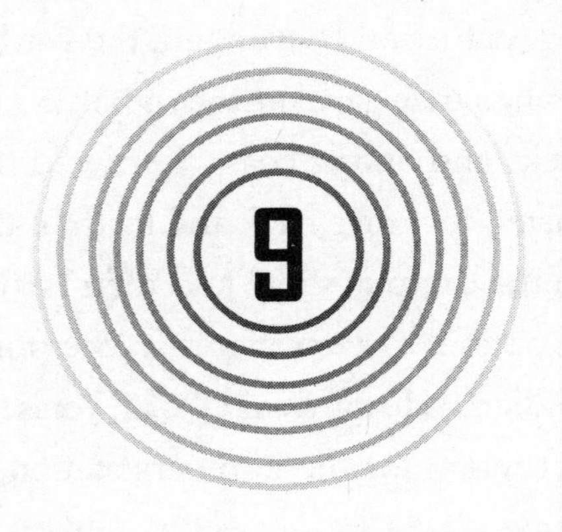

ROBOTS AND RADIOS

BY THE TIME WE GOT HOME FROM BOATING, WE BARELY HAD TIME TO shower and change before we were supposed to meet Elana Mero, the Guidant CEO, for dinner at one of the campus's fancy restaurants. When we were all dressed and ready, we convened in the entrance hall of the town house to head to dinner. Dad looked us over, which I thought was a little funny, given that he's not exactly known for his fashion sense. Savannah was back in her daisy-print dress, I'd donned the A-line skirt Mom had bought for me as well as a ruffled top, and Eric wore khakis and a polo shirt.

"Hmm," said Dad, polishing his glasses against his sleeve. "We seem to be down a man."

Eric rolled his eyes. "He's upstairs writing down numbers again. Turns out the tablet in the room gets local radio."

"What?" Dad asked.

"There's a numbers station in Eureka Cove," I said. "At least, Howard thinks so."

"A numbers station?" Dad said. "And Howard's upstairs, trying to break the code?"

"Yeah." I shrugged. "I told him it was impossible—"

"Don't say that, Gillian," Dad chided me. "Let's go talk to him."

Upstairs, we found Howard in the room he was sharing with Eric. He was seated at the desk, scribbling down numbers as fast as the flat female voice said them. The string of digits eventually gave way to another creepy recitation of a nursery rhyme.

Mary had a little lamb.
Its fleece was white as snow.
And everywhere that Mary went,
The lamb was sure to go.

The voice stopped, and Dad spoke up. "Howard. It's time to go."

Howard started in his seat. "I have to write these down."

Dad nodded. "I understand. But there's an easier way to do this, you know." He came over to the tablet, set on a stand on the desk, and tapped the screen. "Just set it to record. This is how we used to make mix tapes, back in the old days." With the press of a few buttons, Dad set up the tablet to record all transmissions from the station until we got back.

"Oh," said Howard blankly. "I should have thought of that."

"Great. Dinner?" Dad clapped his hands together. "You can tell me all about this station you found on the way. I used to have quite an interest in numbers stations, you know."

I opened my mouth to remind Dad that it was Dr. Underberg who'd tipped us off to this one, but I saw him rest his hand on Howard's shoulder and steer him down the stairs. Message received. We'd talk about it in the car.

As soon as the self-driven car arrived for us, Eric claimed the driver's seat again. Savannah sat shotgun and the rest of us squeezed into the back.

"I think this is really made for four," Dad said, chuckling. Eric gave directions to the car.

"So," Dad said, clasping his hands in his lap. "Numbers stations."

"And codes." I nodded eagerly at Howard. "Just like in the book."

Dad frowned. "That's right. What did the message in the code book say again?"

"'I believe this will soon be useful to you. Good luck,'" Howard and I said at exactly the same time.

Savannah gave me a look. Eric appeared to be choking on something.

Dad pursed his lips. "It does seem a strange coincidence that you were given a book on codes . . . even on numbers stations, and then found one here in Eureka Cove. Then again, there are lots of numbers stations, all over the world."

"What are they for?" Savannah asked.

"No one really knows," Dad said. "Though, of course, there are a lot of theories. Some people think they're communication systems for spies to send instructions, or even just an elaborate prank."

"Or aliens," said Eric.

"Why would aliens need radios?" asked Howard seriously.

"Why would spies?" Eric replied.

"They're basically untraceable," Dad said. "Someone with a shortwave radio broadcasts a signal. Only the recipient knows what it means, but no one knows who the recipient is or where he might be listening. There are probably some you can access back home, and if not, you can pretty much get recordings from any of them on the internet. Ham radio enthusiasts record the transmissions, just like we're recording the one in your room, and then put them online."

Untraceable? I sat back, deflated.

"When we get back to the town house tonight, I want to see that book," Dad said to Howard.

It was silent in the car for a minute.

"Okay," Dad said at last. "Before we get to dinner, I'd like to hear this numbers station of yours."

Eric turned to the control panel. "Play the radio on the numbers station."

The oddly flat female voice started up again. "*Forty-four, twenty-two, thirteen, twenty-four, forty-three, twenty-two, forty-five, thirty-one, thirty-four, forty-one, twelve, thirteen, fourteen, twenty-two, forty-one, twenty-five, thirteen, forty-four . . .*"

"This is why it's better to record these things for later," Dad said. "It can get exhausting trying to write it down and make sure you've got it right."

After another minute of numbers, the nursery rhyme came.

Mary, Mary, quite contrary,
How does your garden grow?
With silver bells and cockle shells,
And pretty maids all in a row.

"Ah," said Dad. "Now, that's a new wrinkle. Is it the same nursery rhyme every time?"

"No," said Savannah. "She was doing 'Twinkle, Twinkle, Little Star' earlier today."

"Then it seems likely to me that the keyword to the cipher is somehow embedded into the nursery rhyme."

"You mean there's a word in each rhyme that works as the keyword?"

"Possibly," said Dad. "And the people the code is meant for know which one it is. Say it's always the seventh word. Or maybe it's the rhyme itself that holds a clue. Maybe the keyword is Mother Goose or something. Or maybe it's the word before the question mark. In 'Twinkle,' that would be 'are,' but in 'Mary, Mary, Quite Contrary,' it would be 'grow.'"

I thought about that. Earlier, in Howard's room, the rhyme the station had used was "Mary Had a Little Lamb." There was no question mark in that rhyme.

"The possibilities are endless," Dad went on with a sigh. "And if they keep the messages as short as they are, there's little chance of using letter frequency theory to help you decode them. If they even are in English. That's what makes number codes such an enduring mystery. I have friends who study them full-time."

"Your friends are weird, Dad," Eric said. "You know that, right?"

"Look who's talking," Savannah said to him.

"Oh, you mean because we're friends?"

Savannah raised her eyebrows. "We are?"

The car pulled to a stop in front of the restaurant. "Remind me to lend you a book I have in my library on numbers stations, Howard," said Dad. "They really are a fascinating field of study, if a frustrating one."

He leaned across me and opened the car door. When Howard made no move to unbuckle, Dad smiled at him and said, "We're recording it, remember? You'll have plenty of time to look at the numbers when we get home, I promise."

Howard seemed satisfied and followed the rest of us onto the street. We watched our car zip off into the gathering darkness, and I wondered if the people who lived here full-time ever really got used to it. When you sat in the backseat, it wasn't too different from riding in a normal car with your parents, or even a taxi or a bus. It was only once you got out, and the car kept going, *all by itself,* that the true weirdness of the situation hit you.

Turns out, Eureka Cove had much more weirdness in store.

Inside the door of the restaurant, instead of the usual hostess stand was a small silver robot that came up to my waist.

"Do you have a reservation?" it asked, as lights blinked

on what could only be described as its head.

"Cool!" cried Eric. "R2-D2 is going to show us to our seats!"

Dad pressed his palm against the panel on the top of the robot.

"Dr. Sam Seagret," the robot said now. "Right this way, please." Then it spun in place and wheeled off into the restaurant, leaving us, openmouthed and stock-still, in the entryway.

"Let's try to keep up," Dad said, and marched off behind it.

The little robot weaved in and out of tables, which was when we noticed that the place, though filled with Guidant employees eating, seemed to have no waiters of any kind. Instead, a whole fleet of robots moved from table to table, taking orders and bringing dishes.

"This is amazing," Savannah said as she passed a robot carrying at least seven plates on his outstretched, tray-like arms. "But I wonder how they know you need a refill."

"You may request a refill, replacement, or other adjustment to your meal using the table-side tablet, and an automated server will bring it to your place setting," said our host robot. It had brought us all the way across the main dining floor of the restaurant and to a set of doors in the wall. "The rest of your party is waiting beyond these doors. Please let me know if I can be of any further assistance."

Eric smirked. "Does it accept tips?"

"Automated servers do not accept tips," the robot replied. "Unless they come in the form of batteries."

"Nice!" he said. "They programmed him with a sense of humor."

Savannah sniffed. "You thought that was funny?"

Eric turned to her. "Aww. You want them to reprogram you?"

10

GREEN DINNER

DAD OPENED THE DOOR TO THE PRIVATE ROOM, REVEALING THREE PEOPLE sitting at a large carved table. Dani, of course, we recognized. There was also a tall man with gelled hair swept back from his face, who rose to his feet as we entered.

"Sam!" he called. "Good evening. And you brought the children!"

Of course he did. That's why there were five empty chairs at the table.

The man waved to us. "Hello, kids. I'm Anton Everett, vice president of sustainable development here at Guidant."

"Hi," we all said, looking up. I didn't know if Guidant had a basketball team, but if it did, he'd definitely play center. He even towered over Dad.

"And I'm pleased to introduce you to Guidant's CEO, Elana Mero."

I'd seen her picture before, of course. Elana Mero was in the news easily as often as other tech superstars like Bill Gates or Mark Zuckerberg. She was definitely older than my mom, but not quite as old as my grandparents. Her hair was pale, and cut in a short and sleek style, and she wore a simple white linen suit jacket with a matching skirt and no jewelry. As she extended her hand to shake my father's, her eyes were on us.

"This must be Gillian," she said, nodding at me. "And there's Eric, so you must be Howard, and that makes you Savannah. What an absolute pleasure. I would have recognized you anywhere from your photo in the book. But where is Nate?" she asked in dismay. "I was hoping to get a chance to meet him as well."

"He had a college visit," Savannah volunteered.

"I mentioned that Nate Noland left the campus, Elana," Dani volunteered.

"Ah." She frowned. "What a pity. When I was forced to skip your visit with the engineers this afternoon, I didn't realize that would be my only chance to hear his version of events. But please, make yourselves comfortable." She gestured to the chairs and we sat.

After we ordered drinks and appetizers from the

tablet, Elana began asking us questions about our trip to Omega City. She wanted a full account of Eric's and my scuba-diving trip through underwater parking garages and up elevator shafts. She marveled at Howard's presence of mind to use an emergency flare to temporarily blind the people chasing us, and she was wild to hear how Savannah managed to navigate the flooded chambers after her arm had been broken in a fall from a catwalk.

A robot came with food and drink as Savannah was relating the story of getting trapped in a room while the floodwaters came in.

"I was all turned around, and separated from Gillian. It was dark and I couldn't find my way out, and didn't know if I'd be able to swim to the exit with my arm. There was nothing but a tiny pocket of air on the ceiling." She smiled at me across the table. "But Gillian found me. She convinced me that if we just got out into the hall, the current would carry us to the stairwell where the boys were waiting. She saved my life."

The adults at the table all looked at me, and I stared into my soup.

"Amazing," said Anton. "Your children are truly extraordinary, Dr. Seagret."

I felt my cheeks heating. None of us really knew what to say. Eric was the first to get it together. "Thank you. And we . . . we really love this campus. The self-driving cars are so cool. And the robots, and the smart courts . . ."

"We think of the campus as a giant laboratory," said Anton. "We aim to provide not just a technologically advanced way of life here, but a sustainable one, too. We're striving for a zero-carbon output. Our homes and buildings are all certified green, and we use water reclamation and solar and wind power wherever we can."

"Anton's special field of development is environmental engineering," Elana explained. "He's trying to save the planet."

"I'm trying to save *humanity*," Anton corrected. "The planet will go on. I'm not sure about humans, if we don't get our act together."

"That was one of Dr. Underberg's big fears, wasn't it, Dr. Seagret?" asked Dani. "That humans would cause their own destruction?"

"It was," Dad said, putting down his fork. "It was like we were discussing this afternoon. He was very concerned about our survival as a species. I'm sure he'd love your Capella satellite."

"Ah," said Elana, taking a sip of her wine. "One of *my* pet projects. Do you really think he'd like it? Sometimes I wonder. . . ."

"Pretty big pet," Eric mumbled under his breath. He was right. It must have cost a fortune to put a satellite into space.

"Of course. Underberg was driven by a desire to help save humanity from disaster," Dad said. "That's why he built Omega City. That's why he became involved with the Arkadia Group . . . those people who call themselves Shepherds."

"Hmm," Elana said thoughtfully. "So if Dr. Underberg was a Shepherd, then they can't be all bad."

"He said joining the Shepherds was one of the biggest regrets of his life!" I argued.

"What else did he tell you about them?" Elana asked.

I was taken aback. "Not much. He took off in a rocket right after."

"Pity." She shrugged.

"It is," said Dad. "Since they're so secretive, it's difficult to do any research on them. The Arkadia Group was the only public face of their organization, and they seem to have disappeared years ago."

"Another pity," Elana said, and actually looked sincere.

I was baffled. I thought she'd read Dad's book! "Don't *you* think the Shepherds were evil?"

"It's complicated, honey," said Dad. "Their aim is supposedly to protect humanity, like a shepherd protects a flock of sheep."

"Okay." That was good, right? That was why Dr. Underberg had joined.

"But they believe that, as a group, we're unable to save

ourselves without someone watching over us. That we're sheep—too meek, too focused on our own little blades of grass to see the wolf in our midst."

"There's a lot of value to that argument," said Anton. "Environmental studies look pretty grim these days. Climate change has reached a tipping point, ocean life is dying off at a huge rate—we're heading toward a catastrophe, and that's not even including the type of danger the Capella project is trying to help us avoid."

I bit my lip. This was a pretty serious conversation for dinner. Dani looked nervously from Anton to us, as if worried he'd be giving us kids nightmares or something. Savannah had already checked out. She was eating impossibly tiny bites of her eggplant. I guess saying she was a vegetarian was easier than actually eating like one.

"And there doesn't even have to be a single cause," Anton said. "There have been several great extinctions in the history of life on this planet, and we know of only one that was definitely caused by a cosmic event—an asteroid striking Earth. And despite what you see in movies, we've got no plans to help us survive such a horrible future."

I shivered. Suddenly, I wasn't so hungry anymore. "Well, there's Omega City."

Dani shook her head. "It was a good idea, but it's gone."

"But Fiona and the Shepherds . . ." Eric looked as

confused as I felt. "They were the ones who tried to destroy Dr. Underberg and discredit my father."

"That doesn't mean they're wrong about the Earth," Anton argued.

I caught myself shaking my head. No! They couldn't be right. If they were right, it meant Dr. Underberg was wrong.

Except Dr. Underberg had been a Shepherd once, too.

My head started to hurt. So the Shepherds were right, but they were evil, and Dr. Underberg was right, but he'd been wrong to be a Shepherd. . . .

"The problem," said Howard slowly, "is that people aren't sheep."

"Exactly," said Dad. "We aren't sheep, and we shouldn't be treated like we can't make our own choices."

"What would you rather be?" asked Anton. "A live sheep, or a dead lone wolf?"

Savannah raised her hand. "I just want to be a person."

"If the human race is to survive, we have to give it as many places to do it as possible. We should have colonies in space, on the moon, on Mars."

"Yes," Howard agreed, nodding wildly. "I'd love to go to Mars."

"Mars isn't quite ready for you, Howard," Dani said.

"Mars isn't ready for anyone," Elana said. "That's the

problem. And unless the people on this planet start taking the threats to our survival seriously, we'll be the ones going down with the ship."

"You mean from an asteroid?" I asked. "One of those extinction-level things?"

"Yes," said Elana. "Could happen any moment, with little or no warning. And what do you think would happen then, Gillian? We'd have nowhere to run to."

Not even Omega City.

"Isn't it sad," mused Anton, "that it would take such a sensational event to wake humanity up to its own fragility? When the scary truth is, we're already in the middle of a great extinction."

"We are?" asked Eric.

Elana raised her hand in defense. "Please, Anton, not another dinner discussing colony collapse disorder."

"What's that?" I asked.

Dani and Elana sighed in unison. "It's bees," Dani said. "There's a major, worldwide problem with bee populations right now."

"And no one knows what is causing it," Anton said. "Pesticides? Cell phones? Sunspots?"

"I think it's Wi-Fi," my father said. "I actually teach a section on this in my seminar Top Ten Mysteries of the Aughts."

"All we know is bees are leaving the hive and not coming

back. When bee colonies collapse, it has major ramifications on our food-supply chain. This is what I'm saying. The population at large does not realize how delicate our entire system is. How one tiny problem, as minuscule as a bug, could send the whole thing crashing down."

"Don't worry, Anton. For now, the bugs are under control." She forced a smile as Anton sat back in his seat, chastened; then she turned back to us. "Tell me about your day. Where did you go on campus after the tour?"

"We went to Eureka Cove," Eric said. "We took out a powerboat to go tubing."

"Oh, how fun," said Elana. "It's been quite a while since I got a chance to go out on the water. The weather was beautiful for it today, wasn't it?" As she spoke, the robots entered again to clear our plates and bring in our main dishes.

"Yeah," Eric agreed. "Though I have to tell you, the self-driving boats don't work quite as well as the cars."

"No, that's true," said Elana. "It's an ongoing problem. See, with cars you have things like lanes and brakes. Boats are much more complicated to program."

"It also kept steering us too far away from the docks and then cutting off," Savannah said. "Why would it steer toward the proximity limit or whatever if it's not supposed to go that way?"

Elana frowned. "It's not supposed to do that. How odd.

Are you sure you didn't command it to steer in that direction?"

I looked down as the robot placed a big plate of pasta in front of me. "We might have," I mumbled to the pasta. "We were talking about radio stations, and I think it was trying to steer us to the radio station on the island."

"No." Elana dismissed that and took a sip of her wine. "The boats are only programmed to direct you to accessible locations. And anyway, that's just a cell tower relay on the island, not a radio station."

"Nothing on the island was even marked on the map," Eric pointed out.

"That's because there is nothing on the island," Elana said.

"I saw buildings," I blurted. "The tops of ones, anyway."

"Right," Elana said. "I should have clarified. There's nothing *occupied* there anymore. At one time, we used the property for some of our agricultural projects, but it became too difficult to maintain, especially once we committed to our green energy policy. We moved everything back to the mainland."

"So if there isn't a radio station on the island," Howard began, "then where are the broadcasts coming from?"

I kicked him under the table, as if that had ever done any good.

"What broadcasts?" Elana asked.

"The numbers station."

All three Guidant employees stared at Howard, bewildered.

"A numbers station?" Dani asked, amused. "Delivering code in the midst of the biggest data encryption company in the world? That sounds . . . quaint."

"You'll have to forgive us," said Dad. "You know my background is in twentieth-century spying techniques. I've been telling Howard here all about the use of shortwave, coded radio stations in Europe during the Cold War. It's a new hobby of ours."

Yes, a very new hobby. But hopefully Howard wouldn't bring up the code book. It was clear Dad wasn't ready to mention it to anyone else.

"Ah," said Elana, shrugging. "Well, if there's a radio station broadcasting nearby, this is the first I've heard of it. Maybe it's a side project with some of our engineers. They're always getting up to something. Last year they built a robot that could toss a Frisbee and tried to get it on our intramural Ultimate team."

"We actually had to make it an official company policy that all sports team members were made of fifty-one percent human material." Dani laughed, and the tension was broken.

As dessert and coffee were served, the conversation

turned back to Omega City, and our adventures there. "It all seems so extraordinary," Elana said. "Who knows what we might have discovered if it weren't for Fiona and her dynamite?"

"It was mostly ruins," Eric said. "A lot of run-down buildings."

"And working rocket ships," added Dani. "And batteries. And utility suits."

"Treasures don't have to come in giant packages, Eric," said Elana. "Trust me, I made my fortune in microchips. Which leads me to my next question. You see, I've read your book very carefully, Dr. Seagret. All your books, actually. And so I have a favor to ask."

I exchanged glances with Eric. Here it was. She wanted the battery, just like he'd thought.

But I was wrong.

"I like people with vision," said Elana, "and you have it. You, and your lovely family. How would you like to come work for Guidant?"

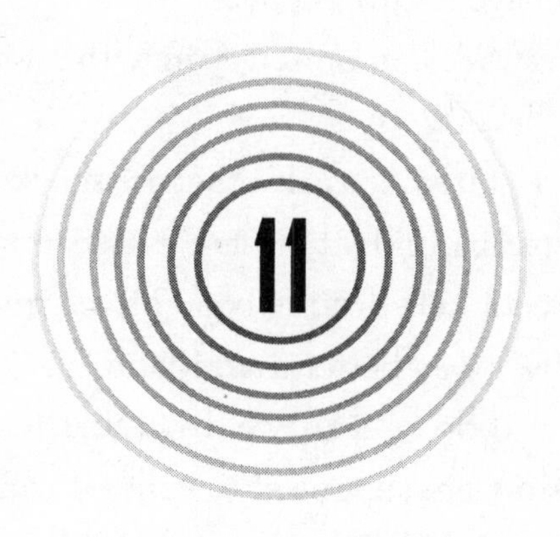

11

SAVVY SECRETS

MY HEAD POPPED UP, AND I ALMOST CHOKED ON MY MARASCHINO cherry.

"You have a place for a history professor?" Dad asked, chuckling.

"How can we engineer the future without understanding the past?" Elana said. "Think about it. You could teach classes and research your next book—this thing about the Shepherds you mentioned. It would come with a salary commensurate to your experience in academia, as well as a full benefits package and, of course, our standard invitation to live on campus."

Dad dropped his spoon into his tea.

"I . . . I'll have to think it over."

"Of course. We can present you with a formal offer in the morning."

Eric and I stared at each other in shock. A full-time job? And here at Guidant, where everything was robots and cars and cool, self-driving boats? Even my brother had to agree that was way better than Idaho.

Though it didn't mean we'd be able to come along. Mom and Dad were supposed to split custody of us. Dad had us last year, so Mom was supposed to have us this year. And that probably meant we were going to Idaho, whether we liked it or not.

"The children can attend our schools here. We have a wonderful program. Very self-guided, very flexible, to give them a chance to pursue their passions." She looked at Eric and me. "They're such bright, curious kids. I think they'd really thrive with our innovative learning techniques."

"Well," Dad said, "I'm not sure if—"

If we'd even be in the state.

"You see, my ex-wife is supposed to have custody of the children this coming fall," he finished.

"Yeah," I grumbled. "In *Idaho*." Hard to practice "innovative learning techniques" when you bounced back and forth between parents every other year.

"Oh, dear," said Elana as she scooped up some ice cream. "Idaho is so cold. Trust me, Gillian, Eureka Cove is a much more comfortable choice."

I shook my head. If only it were one I got to make.

AFTER DINNER, ELANA wanted to take Dad, me, and Eric on a quick tour of the campus in case we moved here. Eric seemed fine with the idea, which I didn't understand, seeing as how he'd been totally in support of Mom's Idaho plan.

"What does it matter?" I grumbled to him as I watched one driverless car take Savannah and Howard back to the guest house where we were staying. "If we're not even going to be here."

"Cheer up, Gills," Eric shot back. "I don't think the Earth is about to be destroyed by a comet quite yet."

"That's not what I meant and you know it," I said as the next car arrived for us. I climbed in the backseat with him, while Elana and Dad took the front. "I'm talking about us living with Mom next year."

"This isn't just about next year, though," Eric said. "This could be Dad's whole future. I wouldn't mind spending every other year here. And summers, and vacations . . ." He gazed out the window happily. I'm sure he was already imagining a boat in the cove with his name on it.

But I couldn't get excited. Eureka Cove was awesome, but bouncing back and forth between here and Idaho like a pair of Ping-Pong balls? When would I get to see Savannah?

These thoughts filled my brain as Elana showed us the schools and the shopping district. Finally, we arrived at the staff residences and the car pulled up to a brightly lit home on the first street.

"Here we are!" Elana announced, and we disembarked. Above us, the midnight-blue sky twinkled with distant stars as a breeze wafted gently through the manicured trees flanking the front stoop.

"You leave the lights on in an empty house?" Eric asked. "I thought you guys were into saving energy."

"I had them turned on before we arrived," she answered, and pointed toward the roof. "And look: solar panels. The power you see comes from renewable resources like solar. But thanks for keeping me honest, Eric."

She started pointing out other features as we walked through the house, which looked like a slightly larger version of the town house where we were already staying. In all honesty, the tour was pretty boring. Even my father looked like he was just nodding along politely as Elana showed off the exact appliances and other amenities that we'd already seen when we'd first arrived at Eureka Cove.

"So these are all Guidant prototypes?" Dad asked as we stood in the kitchen.

"Prototypes, yes," Elana agreed. "Except for the products we already have on the market. I've found that my own employees are the best beta testers there are. In fact, the whole idea of having the bulk of my workforce live on campus was to test-drive the technologies I hope to put in every household in the world."

"I'd hold off on those toilets," Eric mumbled.

"Oh, the toilets are already on the market," Elana said with a wave of her hand. "They work perfectly well if you follow the instructions. Trust me, Eric, we have much buggier experiments going on. But for every miscalculation, residents of Eureka Cove get half a dozen wonderful new technologies before anyone else. Drone delivery systems, robotic service staff, driverless cars, smart shopping . . ."

"Smart shopping? What's that?" I asked.

"It's a pilot program here on campus," Elana explained. "When residents of Eureka Cove buy things, they don't use cash or credit cards but instead their handprint, which is directly linked to their employee account. That way, we have a running data stream of what they purchase and where they purchase it. We know if you usually buy a banana every day at your school cafeteria. When we know how many bananas get bought, we can make sure the cafeteria knows, too, so they can always order the right amount. You won't have to worry about the stores running out of items you need, and the stores won't have to worry about wasting money on ordering too many."

"Cool," Eric said, but Dad looked appalled.

"And that's not all. If, after we start mapping your

preferences, you *stop* buying bananas, we can contact you to see if you just forgot for a day or if you'd rather we started stocking apples instead."

Dad shuddered—this time I was sure of it. "Sure," he said, "it's all fine when we're talking about bananas, Eric. But this is really about privacy. I'm sure you can think of a lot of things you might want to buy without having your employer know about it. And when you add in that they know where and when and how much you're buying . . ."

Eric's face turned pink, and I realized that I could think of certain things I didn't want anyone to know about, either. Was this really how everyone in Eureka Cove bought things?

"Yes," Elana admitted. "The privacy issue was a concern to our employees at first, too. It's sometimes hard for people to grasp the value of progress."

"Or maybe they don't see it as progress," Eric muttered.

"But"—she smiled in triumph—"they soon saw that the convenience of the system far outweighed any perceived invasion of their privacy."

"*Perceived* invasion?" Dad echoed. "You're keeping track of their schedules, their diets, you're emailing them to quiz them about casual preferences—"

Elana wagged her finger at him. "That's why I like you, Dr. Seagret. You aren't afraid to express your opinion.

I don't want to surround myself with yes-men who agree with me just because of who I am. You have no idea how hard it is, when you've reached my level, to find people who will give it to you straight. And I need my team to be made up of true visionaries."

"Visionaries you can keep tabs on?"

Elana's mouth snapped shut, and she seemed to consider this for a moment. Finally, she spoke. "I can understand how this must be a sensitive subject for you, Dr. Seagret, given your experiences."

Dad narrowed his eyes. "What do you know of my experiences, Ms. Mero? Have you been collecting data on me, too?"

Eric and I exchanged glances. Maybe we wouldn't have to worry about where we'd live on campus after all. The last time Dad thought someone was keeping tabs on him, we all wound up staying in a tent and boiling our drinking water.

She straightened. "I can see I've hit a nerve, and I'm sorry. I truly believe this is a misunderstanding." She looked at us. "Perhaps we should send the children home, and you and I can sit down and discuss this in detail."

I was pretty sure Dad would turn her down, and that we'd be packed out of Eureka Cove that very night, but soon enough, Eric and I found ourselves in the front seats of one car, heading back to the visitors' town house, while

Dad and Elana Mero zipped off in another.

"Well, that was awkward," Eric said.

"Yeah." I fisted my hands in my lap. "I thought she might take back her job offer on the spot."

"I thought Dad might freak out and make us all go off grid again."

"Me too!" We were quiet for a moment, contemplating this. Even Idaho seemed like a better option.

"Ms. Mero kind of freaks me out," Eric said. "What was all that talk about the end of the world? She's as obsessed as Dr. Underberg."

"Maybe," I agreed. "But she hasn't built a whole underground city." That we knew of, anyway.

"No, but she put a satellite in space just to watch for asteroids," Eric replied. "That's pretty extreme."

I shrugged. Listening to Anton and Elana talk at dinner tonight, it wasn't extreme enough. We could end up going as extinct as the dinosaurs.

Still, there was a difference. Dr. Underberg had built Omega City to save us, in the event of an asteroid or a nuclear war. Even if Guidant did detect an asteroid with their satellite, what could they do? Like Dani said, Omega City was gone, and despite all I'd seen today, it didn't look like Guidant had a plan to save us. Just . . . warn us.

Eric watched the buildings fly past. "Dad's right. I don't like the idea of everything we do being tracked and recorded like that, even if it is supposed to make things more convenient for us. Once you start to think about it, it's creepy."

Never had my brother sounded more like my father.

"They have a record of everything we've done here. Like the smart court and the boats and the cars and stuff. They know what we all ate for dinner tonight. They know how many of us are in the cars or on the smart courts."

"Except when the system doesn't work right," I pointed out. "Like how it didn't notice Howard was on the court."

"Right." We lapsed into silence again.

"But just because they know," I said, "doesn't mean they want to do anything with that information. Or that they're able to."

Though even as I said it, I knew that didn't make it feel any better.

ERIC AND I arrived back at the town house to find Howard shut away in the boys' room, listening to the numbers station, and Savannah locked in the bathroom.

"Are you okay?" I said to the firmly closed bathroom door.

"Yeah," added Eric. "You didn't get eaten by the toilet, did you?"

I gave him a look.

He shrugged. "I'm dead serious. Those things are a menace."

I tried knocking again. "Sav? What's going on?"

"Send Eric away," came a voice from inside.

"Why?" he asked.

"I mean it!" she cried. "Get rid of Eric."

I glared at him, but he just shook his head. "No way. Now I've got to know what's happened."

Throwing back my shoulders, I tried to copy Dad's tone. "Eric," I said, "I'm sure you can think of a lot of things you don't want to know about that may have happened in there."

It worked. Eric went pale, then made himself scarce.

"Okay, Sav," I said, trying the handle. "He's gone. Let me in."

The lock clicked free, and I entered, then gasped.

Savannah sat on the edge of the bathtub, her face glum. Her shirt was off, she had a towel wrapped around her shoulders, and her hair looked like she'd put it through a cotton candy machine. It was a massive blond cloud, frizzing out in all directions. The air smelled strongly of burnt rubber.

"Oh" was all I could think of to say. Yeah, way better that Eric didn't see this. He'd never let Savannah live it down. "What—"

She pointed at the counter behind me, where the hairstyling machine lay in cracked pieces. It looked like Savannah had taken to it with a hammer. "It's that stupid machine! I had it set to loose waves."

Loose *tidal* waves, maybe. I bit back a smile.

"Don't laugh! It almost melted my face off!"

"Okay, okay." I held up my hands. "Can I, um . . . touch your hair?"

She nodded tearfully, and I reached out to the fluffy mass, trying to pat it down. It crumpled like tissue paper beneath the weight of my fingers, and I grimaced. "Is there . . . gel in this? Or . . . cement?"

Savannah whimpered.

"So I guess it's not just the smart courts and toilets that need a little work." I frowned at her hair. "Let's try cream rinse?"

Once I had her head under the faucet and the bird's nest on top of her head lathered up, I told her about the house and the debate Dad and Elana had had over privacy.

Savannah groaned. "Only your dad would pick a fight with Elana Mero the night she offers him a job," she said as I glopped several handfuls of conditioner into her hair and began to massage.

"Well, he has a point," I said.

"So does she—ow!" Savannah yelped as I attacked her with a detangling comb. "People don't always know what they want. How many bananas do you think go to waste in stores all the time? If they knew what everyone wanted, they could stop all that."

"True." I picked up another section of hair. They were obsessed with saving the planet around here. If the smart shopper system worked, they could eliminate wasted products, as well as save on whatever fuel might be used shipping things to the store or hauling garbage away.

"So if people have to sacrifice a little privacy for the sake of the Earth, then I'm all for it," said Savannah. "Think about recycling and composting and all that other stuff. No one likes separating out their recycling. You probably don't remember this because you were only there in summers, but they just started doing recycling back home a year or so ago. And everyone complained at first, but now they realize it wasn't so bad after all. And they're helping the planet. Sometimes people just have to be encouraged to do the right thing."

I tugged out the final snarl and tossed her a towel. "Now you sound like Elana. She said people didn't understand the importance of progress."

"Well, your dad sure doesn't." Savannah patted her hair and surveyed the final damage in the mirror. "This is the best job offer he's had in years, and he's going to blow it."

"So you want him to move to Eureka Cove?"

She pulled her shirt back on and turned to me. "Better here than Idaho, Gillian. At least here you're close enough to visit."

Yeah, but Dad getting a full-time position at Eureka

Cove wouldn't change my parents' custody agreement. I still owed Mom the next year, and she was still moving us out west.

And if Dad took the job, he wouldn't need to keep working on the Shepherd book. According to Mom, that would be better for all of us. We wouldn't be in danger of retribution from the Shepherds for whatever Dad uncovered.

On the flip side, the Shepherds would get away with . . . well, whatever they were doing.

Savannah and I looked at each other in the mirror. Despite our best efforts, her hair was still a mess. As the strands dried, broken bits were sticking out, crimped ends poking up all over her head like straw sticking out of a hay bale.

"What do you think I should do?" Savannah asked.

"Did you bring any hats?"

There was a knock on the door. "Gills? Savannah? Are you two ever coming out of there?"

"He's such a pest," said Savannah. "What is it, Eric?"

"Um . . ." My brother trailed off. "It's the Shepherds. They're here."

CROOKS

I YANKED THE DOOR OPEN. "WHAT DO YOU MEAN, THE *SHEPHERDS* ARE HERE?"

Eric and Howard blinked at us. "Whoa," said Eric. "What happened to your hair?"

"None of your business," Savannah snapped. "And what about the Shepherds?"

"Howard thinks he's translated one of the number code messages, and he says it's about the Shepherds."

"I don't *think* it," Howard corrected. "I know it. The message has to be correct. The chance that I could translate a code that was wrong and also made up a real message is practically impossible. It says so right in the book."

"Show me." If there was one thing Howard was good at, it was solving riddles. Last year, he had been the one to figure out the clues leading to Omega City. Maybe that's why Dr. Underberg had sent him the code book—if it really was Dr. Underberg. We exited into the hall and headed toward the boys' room, Savannah swiping her ruined hair into a messy bun as we went.

Papers covered with grids of numbers and letters in Howard's messy handwriting were strewn all over his and Eric's beds.

"Since we started recording, there have been three transmissions from the numbers station: one after 'Mary Had a Little Lamb,' one after 'Mary, Mary, Quite Contrary,' and one after 'There Was an Old Woman Who Lived in a Shoe.' There were also the two I wrote down earlier today: 'Twinkle, Twinkle, Little Star' and 'Hey, Diddle, Diddle.' And I think it's like your dad said. The codes change with every new transmission."

I looked at the mess. "So you're trying to break all of them?"

Eric jumped in. "There are two options here. One is that the code has a key that only the people the code is meant for know."

"Sort of like the word 'Omega' in the message Dr. Underberg left you in the code book?" I asked Howard.

"Yes," said Howard. "Dr. Underberg knew I'd try that word. An outsider would never think of it. In this case we have no idea who these messages are meant for, so if it's a keyword like that, we'd never be able to break the code."

Eric interrupted. "The other option would be like Dad said—that the keyword was in the message itself."

"So I tried to do that."

"*We* tried to do that," Eric said. "I filled out some of those stupid grids, too."

"We started trying to break the code using every word in every poem."

"Yikes," said Savannah. "That's what you've been doing in here all this time?"

Eric glanced at her hair. "Yeah, who had a better time?"

Savannah went quiet.

Howard handed me a sheet of paper. "But it was all gibberish. Until this one."

I looked down and saw the words "Mary Had a Little Lamb" written at the top, and then, underneath, a grid of numbers and letters.

51	*12*	*15*	*43*	*12*	*15*	*45*	*24*	*51*	*45*
15	*21*	*24*	*55*	*14*	*42*	*35*	*42*	*53*	*15*
42	*41*	*14*	*21*	*45*	*31*	*15*	*14*	*21*	*14*
15	*52*	*45*	*15*	*33*	*21*	*23*	*42*	*53*	*15*

	1	*2*	*3*	*4*	*5*
1	*W*	*H*	*I*	*T*	*E*
2	*A*	*B*	*C*	*D*	*F*
3	*G*	*J*	*K*	*L*	*M*
4	*N*	*O*	*P*	*Q*	*R*
5	*S*	*U*	*V*	*Y*	*X/Z*

"I tried it with 'Mary,' then 'had,' then 'lite'—"

"Light?" I asked.

"L-I-T-E," he clarified. "It's 'little" without repeating letters. Anyway, that wasn't it, either. Then I tried 'lamb'—"

"We get it," Savannah said.

"Well, we made it all the way down to 'white.' When I tried out the cipher with that keyword, we got results."

51	*12*	*15*	*43*	*12*	*15*	*45*	*24*	*51*	*45*
S	*H*	*E*	*P*	*H*	*E*	*R*	*D*	*S*	*R*
15	*21*	*24*	*55*	*14*	*42*	*35*	*42*	*53*	*15*
E	*A*	*D*	*Y*	*T*	*O*	*M*	*O*	*V*	*E*
42	*41*	*14*	*21*	*45*	*31*	*15*	*14*	*21*	*14*
O	*N*	*T*	*A*	*R*	*G*	*E*	*T*	*A*	*T*
15	*52*	*45*	*15*	*33*	*21*	*23*	*42*	*53*	*15*
E	*U*	*R*	*E*	*K*	*A*	*C*	*O*	*V*	*E*

"'Shepherds ready to move on target at Eureka Cove.'" I eyed Howard. "You're sure there's no way this could be an accident?"

Howard shook his head, and a chill stole across my skin. I'd wanted to help Dad with his Shepherd book, but the last time any of us met a Shepherd, it was Fiona, and she'd tried to kill us.

"It's practically impossible," said Savannah. "There's no way that particular sentence could be an accident, or that there would be another way to translate it." She shivered. "What could it mean?"

"There was nothing else?" I asked.

"Nothing that we've been able to figure out yet," said Eric. "Howard just translated this one and then we came and got you right away." He looked proud of himself. "See? I told you I was on your side for the next crazy theory."

Yeah. Except this wasn't crazy at all. "Okay," I said slowly. "We need to figure out the rest, then. And we need to show this to my dad when he comes home."

"But what do we think it is?" Savannah asked. "Why would someone be talking about the Shepherds here at Eureka Cove?"

I stared at the message, but I had no idea. We didn't even know who was sending the messages, or who they were sending them to.

"This doesn't actually say there are Shepherds *here*." I

tapped the page. "This is just an informational message. *Someone* is telling someone else that Shepherds are ready to move on . . ."

"Something," Eric finished. "Some target. So pretty much an utterly useless message for the rest of us."

He was right. The message told us nothing. We had to find out more. "Pass me some paper," I said. "And tell me how to make a grid."

So we all sat down for Howard's crash course on encryption. It wasn't actually that hard, just time-consuming. All you did was make a grid with five numbers across, then five down. Next, you picked a keyword and filled that in on the first line of the grid, then continued with the rest of the alphabet, skipping over the letters that you'd already used in the keyword. After that, it was just a matter of using the key to translate the number strings from the recording.

But even with four of us trying to break the codes, all the other numbers came out like gibberish.

"What do you have?" I asked Savannah after a while.

She rolled her eyes and stared at the paper she'd been working on, something from a recording of "Mary, Mary, Quite Contrary." "'Glbsh vranay, plbmicki enoshka.' That's from 'quite.' You want to hear 'contray'? That's 'contrary' without repeated letters."

"Is it any better?"

"Nope."

Eric was translating lines from "There Was an Old Woman Who Lived in a Shoe" and doing dramatic readings of the nonsense that resulted. We were getting nowhere.

Howard consulted the code book. "What we're doing now is called brute force decryption," he explained. "Trying every possible combination in a methodical way. It's the slowest possible form of decoding there is."

"Oh, goody," said Eric, and started in on a grid that used the keyword *children*.

"So maybe it's something else," I said. "Like . . . 'white' was the ninth word in the poem."

"The ninth word in my poem is 'a,'" said Eric. "Not much of a keyword. Plus nothing happened when I tried it."

"This could be anything," Savannah said. "Maybe the key isn't even in the poem. Maybe the fact that 'white,' the keyword, was in 'Mary Had a Little Lamb' is just a coincidence."

"Or maybe it's another clue," I said. "Have we tried to use the keyword 'white' on any of the other recordings?"

Half an hour later, we all frowned down at the nonsense on our papers.

"Okay," I said. "So it's not 'white.'"

Eric yawned. "Can we start this up again tomorrow, Gills? I'm starting to forget the alphabet." He showed me his latest page, in which he'd repeated the letter L twice in the grid.

I sighed. There had to be something. Howard couldn't have translated that message by accident. And it had to be important, too, otherwise why would Dr. Underberg have sent Howard the book?

I felt like such an idiot. I'd wasted this whole summer worrying about my mother's plans, when there were much bigger problems to solve.

Shepherds ready to move on target at Eureka Cove. The words swirled endlessly around in my head as I tried on different meanings. What if the target was Dad? He was the one they'd targeted the last time he'd started to expose them.

Except Mom had pointed out the Shepherds didn't seem to care at all about his book on Omega City. Maybe they didn't care about Dad anymore.

So then, what were they after?

"What's so important?" I blurted out.

"About white?" Savannah asked, although that wasn't what I'd meant.

"It's a color," Eric volunteered.

True. "Are there any other colors?"

"In life?" asked Howard.

"In the nursery rhymes," Savannah said. She pointed

at her sheet. "Silver bells. In Mary's garden."

"Yes!" We crowded around Savannah as she quickly mapped out a grid for "silver."

But the result was a whole lot more of nothing.

"Whatever the answer is," Savannah said, "we don't have it. Eric's right. We should go to bed."

"I'm right?" Eric repeated incredulously. "Wait. Can I get that on record?"

I stared at the mess of papers. Like I'd be able to sleep with a mystery like this hanging over my head. "It's okay. You guys go to bed. I'm going to keep trying."

"Come on, Gills." Eric put his hand on my shoulder. "Don't be like Dad."

"What is that supposed to mean?"

"You know what it means. Up all night working. We only have one more day here. You don't want to be a zombie tomorrow. There's nothing here that can't wait until morning."

"And in the morning, we can ask Dr. Seagret," Howard added. "Maybe he has a better idea how to test the codes, other than brute force."

I frowned. Don't be like Dad? I wished I were *more* like him. Then maybe I'd be able to figure this out.

THE NEXT MORNING, I woke up the second I smelled coffee burning. It was so good to be back with Dad. Savannah was still sleeping, her head wrapped up in a towel. Before bed last night, she'd done some kind of deep-conditioning treatment to try to salvage what she could. Quietly, I threw on some clothes and headed downstairs.

Dad was in the kitchen, wrestling with a hissing chrome machine. As I got closer, I could see half a dozen multicolored lights blinking at him in protest.

"I don't understand," he said sadly. "I just asked for a cappuccino."

"Here, Dad." I pulled the plug, and everything went dark. After a few seconds, I plugged it back in. It pinged happily, and the words *Guidant Caffeinator* appeared on the readout below the dispenser. "See, to get a cappuccino, you just press this button for hot, then this one for the type of drink, then this one for the size. . . ." I set the machine and put a mug underneath.

Dad chuckled as the machine perked away. "And here I thought automation would save me in the kitchen. It was going to be the best thing about living here."

I whirled around to face him. "You took the job?"

"I could hardly refuse, Gillian. A guaranteed salary, great benefits, a place to live . . ." Dad paused and looked thoughtful for a moment. "And there's something more. Elana and her team—they have a vision. And that's rare these days. They have a vision for the future. I look at them and I see people like Dr. Underberg. People who are truly concerned about the good of humanity."

"That's great, Dad."

The coffee finished perking and I handed Dad his mug.

"Can you set it for cocoa or something?" Dad asked.

I smiled. "Sure." After we were settled at the dining room table with our steaming mugs, I started to grill him. "What happened with all that smart shopper stuff? Aren't you worried about the way Guidant invades people's privacy?"

"I am, kiddo," Dad replied. "And here's the thing: Elana is, too. She listened to all my concerns last night, and shared that a few of the developers are worried also about how this technology could be abused by the people who use it. Guidant wants to help people, but not at the expense of their freedom. That's why the program is in beta."

"What's beta?" I asked.

"It's a term programmers use when they're still working out the kinks in a project. Beta is the second letter in the Greek alphabet. So if alpha is first—the people who make up the program—betas are the second group, who test it and hopefully uncover problems the creators didn't plan for. Like how can shoppers keep their personal information private, while still helping them to get what they need and helping the stores to eliminate waste."

"So until they've fixed the problems from the beta testing, they aren't going to release the project?" I asked.

"Exactly. The people who live and work here at Eureka Cove are the beta testers for everything Guidant invents. For instance, everything that happened with the Noland boys on the smart court yesterday is going to be beta testing for the smart courts."

"They have a lot more testing to do, then," I said.

"But the important thing is that they're committed to doing it," Dad pointed out. "They aren't going to release a shoddy product on the world. That's how Guidant became as large as it is. They don't just want to make money, they want to make a difference. And after listening to Elana and understanding what she wants to do with this company, I want to help."

"As a history teacher?"

"History is important for planning for the future, Gillian. Don't tell me I've taught you nothing!" He flicked the end of my ponytail. "I'll be teaching, yes. But the first project Elana wants me on is actually in my capacity as an Underberg scholar. Guidant is one of the most innovative technology companies on the planet. Who better to produce his inventions?"

"So she does want the battery." My grip on my mug tightened. Mom and Eric had been right. "Did you give her the prototype?"

Dad looked at me. "This isn't like Fiona, kiddo. *Someone* has to produce these batteries, and Guidant can do it very easily. The patent will still be in Dr. Underberg's name, and they can make sure that some of the money goes into a trust that will belong to him . . . if he ever reappears. Or his heirs."

I must have still looked uncertain.

"You know it's not *our* battery, either, right?"

True. And what good was it in our possession, anyway? We weren't engineers.

"Dr. Underberg would have wanted it this way. He'd want his work in the hands of someone who planned to use it to help mankind. I believe that's Elana and Guidant. I'm sure if he were able to contact us, he'd agree."

That reminded me. "But he *is* contacting us. That code book—"

"Right," Dad said. "I did want to find out who sent Howard that book."

"Well, it's gotten more interesting. Howard was working on the numbers station codes last night after dinner. He says he solved one—"

"Oh, yeah. I asked Elana about the station last night. She said her assistant Dani looked into it, and it's one of the projects they're doing at the campus middle school. Decryption is a huge part of tech, and sometimes the school sets up spy games and other projects. Last year it was some sort of geocaching experiment. Howard would have been great at that, too."

"Geocaching?"

"Following GPS coordinates to find items." Dad winked at me. "Like you did for Omega City."

Following GPS coordinates was the easiest part. It was finding out that the coordinates were based on Underberg's riddle that had been hard. I'd like to see the Guidant Middle School kids do that. "But the message said, 'Shepherds ready to move on target at Eureka Cove'! Why would kids doing a school project send messages about the Shepherds?"

"Maybe because everyone here has read *The Forgotten Fortress*," Dad said. "And they are playing a spy game about actual spies."

I considered that. If I were playing a code-breaking game, I'd definitely want to use the Shepherds in it. "You think that's it? They're just playing a game?"

He smiled down at me. "Well, what I *don't* think is that real spies use codes that can be broken by a couple of kids with their first code book. Even if those kids are you." Dad gulped down the last of his coffee. "Nor do I think spies call themselves by name in their secret messages."

That was true. They'd probably just say, *We are ready to move on our target* or something.

"But don't worry, we'll figure out who sent that book, I promise. As soon as we get home. But for now, I've got some meetings with the Guidant people to finalize plans.

You have fun today, okay? Your cell is charged in case you need to call me?"

"Yes, Dad." I didn't move to get up from the table as he departed. Had I kept Eric and my friends up half the night breaking codes that were nothing more than some Guidant Middle School cryptography club game?

Soon after, Eric thumped his way downstairs, bleary-eyed. He grabbed some granola bars and made himself scarce, probably scared that I'd ask him to start code breaking again. Savannah came down later, shaking her mane of glossy blond hair over her shoulder and preening in triumph.

"So the deep conditioning worked?" I asked.

She smiled. "Just remind me to keep it low-tech next time."

I guessed that hairstyling machine was in beta testing, too.

Savannah and I had breakfast, and I told her about my conversation with my father. I'd expected her to be mad we'd wasted last night code breaking, but she shrugged it off.

"It was fun, anyway," she said. "I wish they did projects like that at our school. If you end up going here, you can kick all their butts."

"Not really," I said. "Howard was the only one who managed to break a code all night." Besides, I wouldn't be going to a Guidant school anytime soon. I wondered if they taught code breaking at whatever school Mom planned to send us to in Idaho. "And what about the other stuff? Do you think Guidant might be using Dad to get their hands on the Underberg battery?"

"Using him?" Savannah cocked her head to the side. "How so?"

"Like Fiona."

Savannah frowned. "Fiona was pretending to get close to your father so she could steal his notes about Dr. Underberg and find Omega City and claim the battery as her own."

"Right." So what?

"Well, Guidant is offering your father a house and a job so he can use his expertise on Underberg to help them develop Underberg's battery. That seems like a huge difference to me."

"But they want the battery."

"Yeah," Savannah said, nodding, as if that was obvious. "So do I. We all want the battery. Even if Fiona had stolen it and pretended it was her invention and made a billion dollars selling them, it still would have ended up being a good thing—"

I gasped, outraged.

"Because it would have meant the *world* had the battery."

Hmph. I crossed my arms over my chest. "You know,

Fiona used that exact same argument on me, right before she threatened to kill us all."

"Well, that's not what happened, is it?" Savannah said. "*We* got the battery, but we can't just sit on it forever. I think your dad is doing the right thing."

"You think I'm just suspicious of everyone, don't you?" I said.

"Yes," Eric said, coming in from the backyard. "What are we talking about?"

"Dad's going to help Guidant develop the Underberg battery," I explained.

"Awesome! Then you can stop hoarding ours." He grabbed an apple from the bowl on the counter. Like everything else in the kitchen, it was polished to a bright shine. "Any idea when Howard's getting up? I was hoping we could try the boats again today."

We headed upstairs to wake him, but found him already hard at work at the desk.

"There was another message," he explained without looking up from his papers. "This one was for 'Baa, Baa, Black Sheep.' And I think I figured out where we went wrong last night."

"It doesn't matter," I said, but Howard ignored me.

"Most of the messages are gibberish," he said. "They're there to confuse us. It's not just the code words you have to figure out, but which messages to use them on."

"What do you mean?" asked Eric.

I tried again. "You can stop decoding. Elana Mero told Dad it was just a school project."

But Howard kept talking. "Well, the messages are about the Shepherds, right? So what if the only rhymes that mattered were the ones having to do with—"

"Sheep," Savannah finished. "Like 'Mary Had a Little Lamb.'"

"And 'Baa, Baa, Black Sheep,'" added Eric.

I groaned. "Didn't you hear me? It's just some stupid game. There's nothing important in the messages."

Howard turned around and shoved a paper under my nose. "Wrong."

Like before, the code word was the first five-letter word in the rhyme—in this case, *black*.

44	*22*	*13*	*24*	*43*	*22*	*45*	*31*	*34*	*41*	
S	*E*	*A*	*G*	*R*	*E*	*T*	*I*	*N*	*P*	
12	*13*	*14*	*22*	*41*	*25*	*13*	*44*	*22*	*45*	
L	*A*	*C*	*E*	*P*	*H*	*A*	*S*	*E*	*T*	
53	*35*	*45*	*35*	*11*	*22*	*12*	*13*	*51*	*34*	*14*
W	*O*	*T*	*O*	*B*	*E*	*L*	*A*	*U*	*N*	*C*
25	*22*	*21*	*35*	*34*	*31*	*44*	*12*	*13*	*34*	*21*
H	*E*	*D*	*O*	*N*	*I*	*S*	*L*	*A*	*N*	*D*

Seagret in place. Phase two to be launched on island.

My brother peeked over my shoulder, then gave me a worried frown.

If Dad was the target the Shepherds were after in their other message, what were their plans for him in "phase two"?

Eric was already dialing Dad on the phone. "Straight to voice mail," he reported.

I did not like this, not at all.

"Well, he has that meeting," said Savannah, but she didn't sound convinced.

"Call Elana's office," Eric suggested. "Talk to Dani."

I did, but it wasn't Dani who answered the phone. Instead, the call was rerouted to a receptionist in the executive office.

"Hi," I said to the receptionist. "I'm Gillian Seagret and I'm trying to reach my father, Sam. Do you know if he's supposed to come into the office this morning for a meeting?"

"Hmm . . . ," the receptionist said. "There's no one here. But I can check the car logs and see where your dad last went."

Right. They tracked everything here. "Thanks."

"Hmm," the receptionist said. "I don't have anything logged on Sam Seagret's account this morning. Maybe somebody picked him up, honey?"

"Maybe," I said, and hung up.

Seagret in place. Phase two to be launched on island.

Someone picked him up, all right. The Shepherds.

13

BAA, BAA

THE MORNING SUN BEAT BRIGHTLY OFF THE SPARKLING WAVES OF THE cove and the silver material of our Omega City utility suits. We stood on the quay, holding our suits under our arms—except Howard, of course. Far across the water, the island sat, wooded and silent . . . and waiting.

"You're sure about this?" Savannah asked.

I nodded. "The way I see it, there's only one island, so if the message said something about an island, then this is the island it meant."

"But we already know the boats won't take us there," Eric argued.

"The car didn't take us all the way to the docks," I

pointed out. "And yet here we are."

I hadn't wanted the self-driving car's record to show that it had dropped us off here, so I directed it to the minigolf smart courts, and then we'd walked over. Now that I knew how easy it was for Guidant to monitor the self-driving cars, I didn't want any Shepherds who might be watching to realize we were headed to the island. Even Elana Mero and her super surveillance didn't have a lock on everything that went down at Eureka Cove. Now, at least, we could make it work in our favor.

"You want us to swim all the way to the island?" Savannah asked, skeptical.

"No." I pointed at the inflatable kayaks stacked at the end of the dock. "Not everything in Eureka Cove is high-tech."

"Kayaks?" Eric whined. "Can't we at least use a sailboat?"

"We're trying to keep a low profile," I said.

"Literally," said Howard, zipping the code book into one of his utility suit's waterproof cargo pockets.

"Look," I said as I zipped my cell phone into one of my pockets, "either Dad's right and those messages are just a school project, in which case, yay, we meet a bunch of kids from Eureka Cove and have, like, a code-breaking club picnic or something."

"Really?" Howard perked up. "Is that a real thing?"

"Or they're from the Shepherds and we're in danger." *Dad* was in danger.

Eric made a face at the kayaks, then turned to me. "Did you try Dad again?"

"Fifteen times," I told Eric. "Do you want me to try sixteen?"

His shoulders slumped. "Better save your energy, if you're planning to row all the way out to that island."

Once we were on the water, I realized how right Eric was. The island was much farther away than it had looked from the end of the dock. The land receded behind us, but the island never got closer. My arms started to burn, then went numb.

"Um, Gillian? Are you rowing?" Savannah asked from the front of our kayak.

"Yes?" I looked down at my jelly hands and willed them to move.

Eric and Howard sailed past. "Should have worked out more with Mom and me this summer, Gills. Stroke! Stroke!"

I scowled and started rowing again. After what seemed like ages, the solid green mass of trees and overgrowth on the island resolved itself into a thin strip of beach with a deep piney woods behind. Through the thick foliage, I could just make out the shapes of blocky buildings and metal structures. Here and there, sunlight bounced off hidden glass, and over it all stood a tall, rocky outcrop topped with the unmistakable metal spire of a radio tower.

We pulled the kayaks up to the edge of the beach. The narrow band of sand was strewn with driftwood and debris, and very unlike the pristine, wide expanse of beach across the cove.

Savannah wiped her face with her sleeve. "That was no fun. I'm melting out here."

"You should put on your suit," said Howard. "Cooling level three."

"We should all put on our suits," I said.

"Why?" Eric asked. "It's not like it's camouflage."

"Neither is your red T-shirt, ace," Savannah said.

"I think the suits are invisible on infrared camera," I explained, shoving my legs into my suit. "Maybe because of the temperature controls, or maybe because of the silver material, I don't know. But Howard was invisible to the infrared cameras on the smart courts. And if someone is watching us, it's probably through infrared camera."

"Why do you think that?" asked Savannah.

Eric sighed. "It's because of the bushes. And I hate that I know this."

"What do you mean, the bushes?" asked Savannah.

"What do you mean, you hate that you know this?" I echoed.

Eric rolled his eyes. "The bushes and trees mean they

wouldn't be able to see us with regular cameras. Also, they can monitor the premises even at night." He looked at me. "I told you, I don't always tune out when Dad talks."

Savannah unrolled her suit. "I hate this thing."

Howard helped her adjust the zippers. "You won't say that after you get the cooling system on."

Once we were dressed, with our cooling levels turned to three, we set off into the woods. Though it looked pretty thick from the beach, with a dark canopy of trees over a tangled, vine-choked undergrowth, about twenty yards in, the foliage thinned out and I could see a sunny clearing beyond the trunks and leaves. We fought our way through the underbrush and eventually broke through. Before us was a small, brownish field enclosed by a series of wire fences that divided the space into square paddocks. Beyond the grass was a cluster of boxy, almost windowless concrete buildings nearly eaten by vines, and a large, crescent-shaped crystalline structure that arched as high as the roofs. Everything was old and grungy compared to the glistening, modern technological wonderland of the rest of Eureka Cove.

"Wow," said Eric. "Guidant just abandoned all this?"

"Well, they wanted it more green," Savannah said. "Do weeds count?"

"That's not what Elana meant. She meant they weren't able to fix these buildings to be in keeping with their environmental initiatives," said Howard.

I didn't see any solar panels or smart cars. Then again, I didn't see any roads, either. So far, it appeared to be exactly what Elana had described—a whole lot of nothing.

We approached the fence, and as we did, what looked like a pile of dead grass shifted and started coming our way. We all froze. As it got closer, I saw tiny black snouts and bright eyes emerging from the light brown mass.

"It's . . . sheep," said Eric. "They're . . . sheep?"

Tiny sheep. The creatures were probably no taller than my knee, with thick, shaggy coats that swept the ground as they headed toward the wires that separated us from them.

"Aww, how cute," Savannah said.

"They're so small!" cried Eric, bending over the fence wires. "Who's a widdle sheep?"

"Baa," said the sheep all at once.

Eric snapped back up. "That was . . . creepy."

"Look at this." Savannah pointed at a sign affixed to the fence.

FLOCK 4

SIZE RATING: IDEAL
WOOL PRODUCTION: IDEAL
MEAT PRODUCTION: UNSATISFACTORY
METHANE PRODUCTION: SATISFACTORY

REPRODUCTION RATING: SATISFACTORY
RESOURCE RATING: SATISFACTORY
COMPLETION DATE:

"What's methane?" I asked.

"Sheep farts," said Howard.

Eww.

"There's another sign over here." Savannah jogged over to the next paddock, which was empty. The sheep turned their heads as one to follow her movement, like they shared a brain or something. Was that a normal sheep thing?

"It says 'Flock Three.' The ratings aren't as good. 'Completion date' was back in May."

Eric ran to the paddock on the other side. "'Flock Two.' Almost all unsatisfactories, except for meat production and size rating. Completion back in March."

"Completion!" Savannah echoed sarcastically. "They mean the day they killed them. Poor sheep." She patted one on his woolly head.

"Baa," they all said.

"Do you think they're clones?" I asked. That's what people did, was clone sheep, right? "They all look exactly alike."

"I think that's because they're sheep," said Eric. "Sheep always look exactly alike."

"Do they always move like this?" I asked. "Bleat at the

same time, turn at the same time?"

"I don't know," he said. "Do I look like a shepherd?"

We both stared at each other as we realized what he'd just said. *Shepherds ready to move on target. Phase two to be launched on island.*

Shepherds.

"Oh, no, Gills," he said. "Don't tell me we're out here because of some actual, literal *sheep.*"

"No." *No.* I refused to believe that.

"This isn't the school's cryptography club," Eric went on. "It's their 4-H."

"No!" We didn't just get some message about shepherds. We also got one with our name in it. "Elana said this island wasn't in use. So at the very least she was lying."

"Wow, call the cops," Eric drawled. "The head of an enormous company lied to a twelve-year-old about something that was none of her business anyway."

"Or maybe she doesn't know about every single project happening on the campus," said Savannah. "She has a huge international company to run. How is she supposed to stay on top of a few dozen sheep, especially if it is a school project like the numbers station? Maybe she doesn't know about the sheep. Poor things."

"Baa," said the sheep.

"Or maybe she doesn't know about it because it's a Shepherd project," said Howard. He pointed to the sign.

There, in tiny print at the bottom right corner, was the image of a pair of J-shaped shepherd's crooks crossed over a globe. I recognized it instantly, from the bags our utility suits came in, the electrified fences placed around the smoking ruins of Omega City, the faded tattoo scar on the inside of Fiona's arm. It was the symbol of the Arkadia Group.

It was the mark of the Shepherds.

I took two steps back, as if the crooks drawn on the sign were about to reach out and grab me. I no longer needed the cooling setting on my utility suit, as the blood seemed to drain away from my body.

I'd expected to feel vindicated—after all, we'd come to the island looking for proof that the Shepherds were here—but instead, my stomach twisted in knots. A few Shepherds hiding out and sending coded messages were one thing. Paddocks bearing the Arkadia Group brand . . . that was something else.

Just then, a loud buzzing filled the air and two flying drones buzzed over the tops of the trees. The sheep all turned their faces to the sky.

"Hoods up!" I hissed, and pulled the silver hood up over the top of my utility suit. This would be the real test. If the drones were only equipped with infrared cameras, there was a chance they wouldn't spot us.

The drones flew about fifteen feet in the air, buzzing

along until they reached the middle of the paddock housing Flock 4 of the pygmy sheep. A hatch in the bottom of the drones' bodies opened, dropping green pellets all over the dusty field, and then they zipped off toward the center of the island. I breathed a sigh of relief.

"Think they saw us?" Savannah asked.

"Let's not wait to find out."

As a unit, the sheep all turned and trotted over to the pellets, bleating in chorus. As a unit, they all lowered their heads to the earth and began snuffling up the food.

As a unit, Howard, Savannah, Eric, and I all turned to one another. I couldn't see the others' faces behind the visors of the suits, but I'm sure they were as astounded as I was.

"Okay, they are really freaking me out," Eric said.

"Come on," I said. "Let's find out where those drones went." If we followed them to the source, we could discover who was really behind this operation, and see if they had Dad.

We slid beneath the wires of the paddock and waded through the mass of bleating sheep. I had to admit, they were quite adorable, with their tiny little faces and fluffy, matted coats. I didn't know sheep came this small. They definitely weren't lambs, either, but full-grown sheep with thick, fluffy coats and long snouts. I couldn't imagine how cute their lambs would be. They'd probably look like little teacup poodles.

I wondered when their "completion date" was. Savannah was right. Poor things.

"Baa," said one, as a whole mess of poop fell out of its backside near my foot.

Then again . . .

On the other side of the paddocks, the vine-choked concrete walls of the nearest building rose before us. I didn't even see a door through the foliage, and there was no sign of the drones, or anything else.

I sighed. I don't know what I'd been expecting. A nice big window into a room where the Shepherds sat like cartoon villains, twirling their mustaches while my dad was tied to a chair?

Yeah, right.

"I'm going to try Dad again." I pulled out my phone, but there was no reception. I showed Eric the screen. "Didn't Elana say that radio tower was a cell phone relay? If that were true, we'd have a signal now."

Another lie. And now the truth seemed horribly clear. What if Elana had lied to us about everything on the island because it was all one big Shepherd project?

What if Elana Mero was a Shepherd?

THE FIRST ASTRONAUTS

NO. THAT WAS RIDICULOUS. THE SHEPHERDS HAD TRIED TO DESTROY MY father's reputation; they'd made Dr. Underberg disappear and erased all his contributions to science. Ms. Mero and Guidant, on the other hand, had offered my father a job—she'd invited Dad to come speak to them about Dr. Underberg and his city, and wanted to bring his battery to the world. They couldn't be more different.

Right?

But here's what I knew. One: this island belonged to Guidant. Two: this island had the marks of the Shepherds all over it. Three: this island was off-limits, and Elana claimed there was nothing here. So either she had no idea what was happening right under her nose . . . or she'd been lying to us all along.

Either way, things didn't look good.

"We should go back," Savannah said. "I kind of promised your mom we wouldn't go off exploring on our own."

"Too late for that," said Howard.

Back where? To Eureka Cove, where every move we made was tracked, and Elana Mero, possible Shepherd mastermind, had my dad?

What if they were *all* Shepherds? At dinner last night, Elana and Anton and even Dani had been defending the Shepherds, arguing that maybe they weren't as bad as we'd thought. And Anton had said they had a point.

How had we been so dumb?

"If Guidant is somehow involved with the Arkadia Group, we're no safer back there than here on the island," I said.

"I kind of think that's not true," said Eric. "Back on the mainland, we can call Mom."

Mom . . . I remembered what she'd said, about the Shepherds leaving Dad alone because it wasn't Omega City they'd been worried about him exposing. The Shepherds had abandoned Omega City decades ago, but whatever was going on here at Eureka Cove appeared to be happening *now*.

But if they were worried about Dad finding them, why would they bring him here, to Eureka Cove? Why would the Shepherds, of all people, offer my father a job? If they'd wanted to kidnap him, they could have just done it. Instead, they bought us dinner.

It didn't make sense at all.

Howard spoke up. "The messages from the numbers station talked about the Shepherds. They talked about the island. And they talked about your family. That's why we're here. Back on the mainland, they tracked our every move. Here, at least, we have a chance of looking around without them knowing what we're doing."

"Huh," said Savannah. "That's a good point."

"Yeah," said Eric. "Scary, but good."

"Okay," I said. "So we're agreed. We'll go back to the mainland once we've figured out what's going on here." We knew the Shepherds had a presence on this island, but not what it was they were doing. Or why.

Or if they really had my father.

WE CIRCLED AROUND the first set of buildings, looking for a way to enter, or any sign of the Shepherds or the drones we'd just seen feeding the sheep. Howard was arguing that if the animals were being cared for by drones, it was possible that no actual Shepherds ever needed to set foot on the island.

"Drones didn't nail up those signs," said Savannah, and Howard fell silent.

Around the other side, a new building came into

view, and we all stopped and stared at it. This one was short and squat, with curved walls studded with long, high windows. It was shaped like a short, squat ring, and up through the hollow center rose the jagged, shattered remains of what I now realized must have once been a towering glass dome.

I followed the wreckage up, up, up, to where the remains of the dome rose above the tops of the surrounding foliage. Enormous panes of cracked glass dangled from triangular metal support structures, looking like they were held aloft by no more than the vines that crawled up the sides. A bushy green growth like a treetop peeked up from the center of the ruin.

"What is it?" Eric asked in a whisper.

"I think . . . I think it's a geodesic dome," Savannah whispered in reply.

"A what?" asked Eric.

She pointed. "See those metal struts? They form a lattice of triangles to help distribute the weight so it won't collapse."

"But it did collapse," Howard said.

"How do you know this?" Eric asked, looking at Savannah in disbelief.

"I built one out of toothpicks for extra credit in math class last year."

"You did?" He made a face. "I didn't know that was an extra-credit project."

"That's because you could barely handle the regular credits."

I stared at the treetop jutting through the center. It looked too big—too tall and thick—to have just sprouted up in the last few years since the building was abandoned. But this structure—whatever it was—was the largest thing on the island. If "phase two" of anything had been activated on the island, surely it would be here. "Let's check it out."

As we drew closer, I saw a pair of double glass doors. The handles were padlocked together, but the panes of glass had broken and fallen away. I reached the doors and checked the ground at my feet. There was a large pane of crumbled glass with the remains of etched writing in it. I could make out the Guidant logo—a large, stylized gamma symbol—and the following words.

IMPANZ
SEARC
ENTE

"Any guesses?" I asked the others.

Howard unzipped one of his cargo pockets. "I'll get the code book."

"It's not code," said Eric, crouching in the dust. "It's missing letters. This first one . . . I have no idea. But I think the second word is 'search.'"

"Or maybe 'research'?" I suggested.

"Yes! 'Research Center.' Now we just have to figure out what they are researching."

"Chimpanzees," breathed Savannah.

"Huh," said Eric. "I guess that does fit. Good guess."

"No." Savannah nudged him with her foot. *"Chimpanzees."* She pointed and we all looked.

The interior of the building was dim and shadowy, a mess of debris, fallen leaves, and broken office furniture. Overturned desks and cracked tables lay alongside piles of abandoned paper, chalkboards, and computer equipment with tangled wires. Beyond these was the massive space under the dome. At one time, it looked like it was separated from this room by large panes of glass, but those were long gone. The interior of the dome was set up like a zoo habitat, crisscrossed by giant ropes and climbing nets and dotted with plastic buckets and rubber balls around the platforms built into the spreading branches of an enormous tree. And there, hidden among the branches and peering out over the nets, were more than a dozen chimpanzees.

They watched us as intently as the sheep had, their tiny black eyes not blandly interested, like the sheep, but rather sharp and knowing . . . and more than a little hostile. They were scattered all over the dome, large and small. Funny, I'd always thought of chimps as cute and sweet, in movies or zoos or on posters in my science classroom. I'd seen them at zoos, looking through the glass with calm disinterest, used to people moving past their enclosures day in and day out. These animals weren't like that. They were wild.

"What's keeping those monkeys in their habitat?" Eric asked.

Savannah stamped her foot. "They're chimps, Eric. Apes. Do you see a tail? Only monkeys have tails."

"Fine. What's keeping those *apes* in their habitat?" When Savannah said nothing, Eric smirked. "Not so smart anymore, are we?"

Howard stepped over the pile of broken glass and ducked through the door frame. The chimps all arched their necks to look at him.

"Um, Howard . . . ?" Savannah began. "I don't know if that's a good idea. They don't seem friendly."

But when had Howard ever listened to any of us? Slowly, gingerly, he crept across the floor, his legs slightly bent, his arms outstretched. The monkeys—apes—watched him approach but remained motionless. As he reached the concrete waist-high divider that still stood between the observation lounge and the dome, the chimps began to vocalize and lunge at him. Howard stopped.

"I think it's okay," he said, "as long as we stay here and

don't cross into their habitat."

Eric went inside, too, and Savannah and I scrambled after them. "So what's keeping them there?"

Howard shrugged. "Look at this place. It's a wreck. There's glass all over. At least their habitat is in good shape."

"True," Eric admitted. "That tree house thing is amazing."

Savannah gasped, indignant. "You're kidding, right? It's still a cage."

Inside, it was almost too dark to see through the visors of our utility suits. I took down my hood, and Savannah and Eric did so too. The room smelled of dust and rot and excrement. The dirty, cracked windows on the outside of the building shone shadowy light onto the remains of what might have once been top-of-the-line equipment. Long desks were strewn with computer screens and other electronics, all broken to bits. The chimps watched us looking around, growing calm again now that it seemed clear we weren't going to enter their space. I even dared to turn around to see what stood above the bank of windows on the outside wall.

My mouth opened in horror. Tall, narrow alcoves lined the walls above our heads, and in each one stood a skeleton. For a second I thought they were the bleached white bones of humans, but I quickly realized they must be chimpanzees, their remains mounted and on display in full view of the animals inside the dome.

As I stared at the skeletons, I could almost feel the accusatory glances of the chimps on the back of my neck. Was this the result of their "completion dates"? At the base of each skeleton was a small bronze plaque. Part of me wanted to read what they said, and another part just wanted to run.

"What kind of monster imports a bunch of chimps to this island and abandons them here?" Savannah asked, still looking at the live animals.

"They aren't trapped," Eric said.

"You mean just because the doors and dome are broken open?" I said. "That doesn't mean they can leave. Where would they go?"

"Chimps aren't native to the Chesapeake Bay." Savannah looked grimly around the observation room. "Who knows how they're even surviving?" She grabbed one of the folders that, miraculously, still lay on a desk and started flipping through it. "This is why I hate animal research. These apes were bred for research, brought here, and now . . . left here."

"Is that allowed?" I asked. There had to be some kind of rules about animal cruelty and stuff, right?

"I'm pretty sure none of this is allowed," Savannah said. She began flipping through the pages. "'Bone density decay as a factor of orbital duration in utero,' 'deterioration of intelligence quotient to the fifth generation' . . . whatever they've been doing to these chimps, it's not nice."

And I was pretty sure Elana must know about it. This wasn't something that could be passed off as some middle school stunt. This wasn't even a wire fence and some pygmy sheep, which, I guess, technically was some sort of agricultural project. I mean, sheep lived on farms.

But this dome had obviously been built for these chimps. Which meant this island had never been *just* a home to Guidant's agricultural experiments.

It was a cover for Shepherd projects.

But what did the Shepherds want with a bunch of chimpanzees? They were supposed to be guiding humanity, not apes.

Howard was examining the skeletons. "This is wrong," he said. "He's not supposed to be here."

"Who?" I asked.

"Ham." He pointed to the chimp skeleton before me. "This plaque says this skeleton belongs to Ham."

"Who's Ham?" Savannah asked.

"The first chimp in space."

"There were chimpanzees in space?" asked Eric.

"Yes," I said. "And dogs and mice and all sorts of stuff. They tested space travel on animals before they tried it out on humans." And it didn't usually work out too well for the animals.

"Typical," Savannah said with a scowl.

Could that be what the Shepherds were doing? Just like NASA, were the Shepherds trying out things on apes before they graduated to people?

"But it can't be Ham," insisted Howard. "His skeleton is supposed to be in a museum."

"Maybe they loaned it out?" Eric suggested.

"And this one." Howard pointed to the skeleton next to him. "It says it's Enos. He also went to space. The dates are wrong, too. Enos died of dysentery a few months after his mission, but this chimp is listed as being alive until 1974."

What were the chances that there were two different chimpanzees named Ham and Enos? "Are these all space monkeys?"

"Space chimps," Savannah corrected.

"They're all the same *names* as the space chimps, if the plaques are right." He looked at the info etched into the bronze. "And the birth dates are right, too. But nothing else is the way it's supposed to be. I read a whole book about the animal program, and this is not the way it is in the book."

Savannah and I exchanged glances. Well, that answered that question. Nothing was ever the way the books said.

Even, I was learning, the ones by my dad.

Howard gestured to the next skeleton. "That's Minnie. She was in the Mercury program. They bred her afterward. . . ." He trailed off. "Oh . . . that's what that paper Savannah saw is about. The fifth generation. They bred the space chimps to see what would happen to their offspring."

"Oh," we all echoed, and turned back to the apes in the habitat. Now their glares made a lot more sense. They'd been abandoned, here, in the tombs of their ancestors.

"What do we do, Gillian?" Eric asked.

"I have no idea. What do you think, Savannah?"

She looked as baffled as me. "I don't know. Call the Humane Society?"

Tracking down the Shepherds and getting to the bottom of their messages was one thing. After all, we'd found Omega City, and we'd outrun Fiona, too. But dealing with a tree house full of abandoned space chimpanzees? That wasn't nearly so clear cut. I took out my cell phone—still no reception—and turned on the camera. At least we could get proof of what was happening here.

The second the camera flashed, the chimps went wild. They started to hoot and jump up and down, baring their teeth and waving their arms in the air. Eric ducked as a stick whizzed by his ear.

Sticks, unfortunately, were only the start.

Something squished against the arm of my utility suit.

I glanced down and another projectile hit me square on the ear, splattering across my neck.

"Monkey poop!" Eric screamed, and we all ducked as more feces came flying our way.

Savannah didn't bother correcting him this time. Together we crawled behind an upturned desk to protect ourselves as the hail of poop intensified.

Savannah made a face at me. "Yuck!"

I grabbed a spare piece of paper and started wiping at the mess on my arm and face. "I thought you liked animals."

"Yes, *animals*. Not their poop." She cowered as something smacked wetly against the outside of the desk.

"Do they have a stockpile or something back there?" I asked.

"Just be glad it's only poop."

"Tell me that when *you* get hit."

"I'm just saying, poop is a sign of *minor* aggression. They could really hurt us if they wanted to." She wrinkled her nose and fanned her hand in front of her face. "It's in your hair, you know."

I groaned. "I know." What did she want me to do, stick it in a Guidant styling machine?

"Incoming!" Eric cried. He and Howard were hiding beneath another desk, their hands over their faces for protection.

"We know!" Savannah and I shouted back at him.

"No . . ." Eric's eyes were wide with fright. "*Incoming.*"

A big, hairy hand clamped down on the corner of our desk.

We screamed.

The chimp froze. The poop stopped. A second later, one of the chimps began calling out, an ear-piercing, barking cry. The ape on top of our desk vanished. I could hear him scurrying back to the habitat. Then I felt it: a vast, buzzing rumble that shook the floor and every pane of glass still standing in the habitat.

"What is that?" Eric asked. I risked peeking over the edge of the desk.

The tree house had become a mass of activity, with every chimp jumping from branch to branch, crawling down the ropes and over the tangled roots at the base of the trunk. As I watched, they started lowering themselves into a hollow under one of the big, knotted roots. "They're hiding," I murmured. But what were they hiding *from*?

Frantic chimpanzees tumbled over one another, fighting to shove into the hole at the base of the tree. I saw a mama chimp holding her hands out to her baby, who clung, trembling, to one of the large swinging balls. She hooted at the little thing, which was all wide eyes as the rumbling passed.

"I'm going to go out on a limb here," said Eric, "and say that if the chimps are scared of it, we should be, too."

"Hide," hissed Howard, and scooted back into the shadows under his desk. Out of the corner of my eye, I saw movement at the door. We flattened ourselves against the furniture. Boots crunched glass somewhere near the vicinity of my head.

I could still see the habitat. The mama chimp screamed and grabbed her baby, hurrying down the tree with the little chimp clinging tightly to her fur. I saw two figures cluster close to the habitat, but could make out little more than dark pants and military boots.

"That one," said a man's voice. Something arced through the air and hit the chimp, who tumbled, limp, to the floor, knocking the baby free. I clapped my hands over my mouth to hide my gasp of horror. Savannah stared at me, terrified, her eyes running over with tears. Her mouth twisted into a determined grimace. I shook my head at her and mouthed, *Don't move.*

The baby cried out and crawled toward its mother.

"Bag it," said a second voice. One of the figures grabbed the unconscious mama chimp, knocking the baby out of the way. The smaller chimp was sent tumbling, hands over feet, as the figure shoved the mama chimp into a dark blue canvas bag imprinted with the unmistakable logo of a pair of shepherd's crooks crossed over a globe.

The Shepherds *were* here. Not just their signs and symbols. Not just their sympathizers. Actual, real live

Shepherds. Every accusation and dark theory my dad had ever written about them reared up in my mind, and I cowered farther behind the desk.

The sound of the baby's sobs filled the air as the figures departed. We waited a minute or two, then emerged from our hiding places. The chimps were doing the same. One dashed out from between the roots, grabbed the screaming baby, and dragged it back down into the hollow of the tree. I could still hear its plaintive cries.

Savannah looked stricken. "What do we do?"

There was something hard and hot in my throat, and I couldn't get the image of the unconscious chimp out of my mind. Whatever was happening here, we were in way over our heads.

15

RECEPTION

"I THINK WE SHOULD GO BACK," I SAID, MY THROAT TIGHT. I HATED TO admit defeat, but even if the Shepherds did have Dad on the island, we were way outnumbered.

"Seconded," said Eric. "It's like Nate says, once there are guns involved, even stun guns, it's time to go."

After making sure the flash was off this time, I took pictures of the habitat, the mess, and even a few blurry shots of the chimpanzees as they slowly emerged from the base of the tree. If the animals knew to hide when the rumbling started, then this couldn't be the first time the Shepherds had come to steal one away.

And because of their advance warning, we'd been able

to hide, too. They had saved us from the Shepherds, so now we had to return the favor. No matter what else happened, I'd have evidence of the conditions these chimps were living under, and what was happening to them.

I had no idea what that sound meant, though, or where the Shepherds had come from. My first thought was a helicopter, though the rumbling sounded nothing like the chop of helicopter blades. Still, the sound had to be connected to the men's arrival.

I didn't want to stick around to figure it out, though. The Shepherds could come back at any time. We weren't safe here.

"Come on," I said to the others. Savannah was rummaging through some of the scattered papers, and Howard had gone back to staring at the skeletons.

We ran back around the outer buildings and skirted the sheep paddocks, pausing to take more pictures of the signs with their Shepherd symbols. We hurried through the woods toward the beach, while Savannah kept chattering about animal testing.

"The truth is, there's probably very little anyone can do. I mean, these experiments are obviously secret, but even if we report the Shepherds, or Guidant, or whatever, the worst that will happen to them is a fine and maybe forcing them to fix their habitat so there isn't broken glass everywhere. The apes still belong to them, so they can stun them or kill them or abandon them or whatever they want. That kind of stuff happens all the time."

I shuddered.

"That's assuming that we *can* report them," said Eric. "The last time someone attacked the Shepherds, it was my dad. And it didn't go so well for him, remember?"

I was quiet, thinking this over. Yes, last time the Shepherds had gone after Dad. But as Mom had pointed out, they seemed much less worried about what Dad was exposing lately—as if Omega City wasn't the problem at all. And if that was the case, then what was it that they were scared of us exposing? What were they doing to these chimps, to these sheep, that was worth keeping everything on this island a secret?

The beach came into view, and we quickened our pace. My arms were still aching from our earlier trip across the cove, but I couldn't wait to get back to the water—and not just so I could rinse the monkey poop out of my hair. As soon as my phone got a signal, I was calling Dad, Mom, everyone. All of a sudden, getting tracked everywhere I went didn't sound half-bad.

There were the kayaks, right where we left them.

And standing in front of them, with their backs toward us, were half a dozen Shepherd guards.

"Stop," I hissed, and dropped to the ground. The others thumped low around me.

"Now what?" Eric whispered to me as I peeked through the underbrush at the knot of men and women clustered around our only means to get home. Like the Shepherds in the ape habitat, they were wearing dark pants and boots, as well as crisp button-down shirts, vests festooned with pockets, and black baseball caps. From a distance, they looked like any security team, complete with utility belts featuring weapons I was afraid to examine too closely. Was one of these guys the man responsible for knocking out that mama chimp? What had they used? Tranquilizer darts? Electric shock? I seriously doubted they'd hesitate to use the same methods on us.

I pursed my lips and thought. Okay, maybe we should have hidden the boats. Of course they had patrols on a forbidden island.

"Wait them out?" Savannah suggested.

I shook my head. Not likely. They weren't talking or anything, just standing around, like they were waiting for us to come back. I supposed that would be easier than trying to find us in all these trees.

So, the kayaks were out. There was no way to swim home. And forget about washing off the monkey poop in the cove.

I pulled out my cell phone, but it still showed zero bars. "If only there were a way to get a message out," I whispered.

"There is," Howard said, taking the phone out of my hands. He pointed back toward the buildings and the cliff. "The radio tower."

"What do you mean?"

"I still have the radio in my room back on the campus tuned to the numbers station, and it's set to record on the room tablet. If we can get to the broadcast station and send a message to your dad . . ."

"But what if Dad is already captured by them?" *Seagret in place . . .*

"If he's not," said Savannah, "at least we can warn him to watch out."

"The radio tower sends Shepherd messages." I shook my head. "They're bound to be listening to whatever we say."

"So?" Savannah broke in. "They already know we're here."

"They know *someone* is here," Eric corrected. "And they don't know what we know. If we send a message through their own system, they'll know we're onto them. And they might be able to intercept Dad before he can reach us."

I looked at him, surprised.

"What?" Eric shrugged. "I told you. I listen to you and Dad."

Eric was right, of course, but I didn't know what other

option we had. Besides, there was always the chance that someone else would hear the broadcast. Some numbers station fan. The Guidant Middle School's cryptography club. I mean, they probably weren't Shepherds, too.

Right?

And we couldn't stay here. Our utility suits might make us invisible to an infrared camera, but it wasn't going to help us hide from actual people only a few yards away. At least back by the buildings or the radio tower, we might blend in with the metal and other rubble.

Cautiously, we retreated through the woods to the buildings, sneaked past the open area around the sheep paddocks, made a wide berth around the geodesic dome in order to avoid any more issues with flying monkey turds, and arrived at the base of the rocky outcropping. Above us, earth and boulders rose several stories in the air, topped by the crisscrossing metal struts of the radio tower. At the base of the tower I could just make out the corner of the boxy little hut that I hoped was the broadcast station.

"How do we get up there?" Savannah asked. "Fly?"

She was right. There were no steps or anything I could see, and the sides of the cliff were too steep for climbing. "They have to get up there some way."

"They have drones," Howard said. "Or helicopters?"

"Maybe there's a hidden door behind the rocks," Eric

suggested. "Like the one Dr. Underberg built over Omega City."

"That's a great idea!" I said.

Savannah cast a skeptical glance at the cliffs. "You guys do realize how many rocks there are on this hill, right? This will take forever."

"Then we'd better split up. You and I can go this way, and Eric and Howard can go that way."

Savannah made a face. "Actually, I'll go with Eric."

"With me?" Eric asked, incredulous. "Are you feeling okay?"

"Yeah." She shrugged. "Sorry, Gillian. You really stink."

Ugh, did I? I'd been wearing monkey poop for almost an hour now. I guess I'd gotten used to it. I turned to Howard, who was the only one of the four of us still wearing his hood up.

"I don't smell a thing," he said. "Though it might actually be a problem with the suit, to be missing an entire sense. What if there's a gas leak or something?"

"Or what if you fart in your suit?" Eric asked. Howard snickered.

Gross. I didn't have time for this. I clapped my hands to get their attention. "We'll keep the hill on our left, and you guys keep it on your right. If you find the entrance, hurry around to meet us."

"And if we run into the Shepherds?" Eric asked.

I told him the only thing I could think of. "Don't."

AFTER AN HOUR of scrambling over the rocks and searching for a way up the tower, we figured out the flaw in our plan. On the far side of the island, the land dropped away to sheer bluffs, all the way down to the water, far below. I had assumed the hill sloped down to smooth, flat land on all sides. Instead, there was nothing beyond our feet but sheer, golden rock and pounding surf. Far above us, the lights of the radio tower blinked infuriatingly.

"Huh," said Howard. I could only imagine what Savannah and Eric were saying, trapped on the other side of this cliff.

I balled my fists at my side. "I messed up. We never should have come here. I was so full of myself. Like we could figure out the Shepherds' plan just because we found Omega City?" Omega City had been an accident. I thought I was looking for a battery, not a place. But this island was dangerous, guarded. Even the animals wanted to hurt us. I dropped my face in my hands and got a huge whiff of monkey poop. "Ugh. Stupid, Gillian."

Howard stood beside me, silent. For once, I was glad he never looked people in the eyes. At least he wouldn't catch me if I started to cry.

Howard reached out and patted me on the shoulder. "It's okay, Gillian."

"It's not okay," I replied. "We're trapped here." I sat on the edge of the cliff, defeated. "And it's my fault."

"How is it your fault?" Howard sat down beside me. "We all came out here."

"It was my idea. I didn't even have a plan. I just . . . I don't know. I wanted to know the truth." Eric was right. I was just like Dad, willing to sacrifice everything to get to the bottom of a mystery.

"I wanted to know, too. I still do. I want to know why they are breeding sheep, and whether those are really the remains of the space chimps. And Savannah really wants to know what they are doing to the chimps in the habitat. We all came here, not just you."

"And Eric?" Could I at least take responsibility for getting my little brother into this mess?

Howard thought for a moment. "Well, Eric wanted to take the boats."

I couldn't help but laugh at that. "Okay, we're all to blame. Now what?" I gazed down at the abyss at my feet, then narrowed my eyes. From this angle, the cliff shadows solidified, making the rocks look almost painted with long, zigzagged stripes.

I peered closer. Or a ledge. A nearly invisible ledge,

switching back and forth down the side of the cliff. I pointed, following the switchback path up the cliff to where it passed about five feet above our heads. "I think there's a path up there."

Howard arched his neck to look. "You're right. Should we go tell the others?"

I thought about this. It had taken an hour to get this far. Another hour to get back to the others, then get back here, then get up the path . . . and every minute we dallied here meant the Shepherds might find us. "I don't think we have that long. If we get to the top, we'll be able to signal to Eric and Sav from up there."

Howard boosted me up, then scrambled up behind me. As soon as I got onto the ledge, I realized my error, as a wave of dizziness washed over me and I clutched at the wall for support. Not again. This hadn't happened since Omega City. Back then, I'd been underground, and Nate had said I was claustrophobic. But that wasn't it at all.

I was just afraid of getting trapped.

I squeezed my eyes shut for a second. All I had to do was walk. One step in front of the other. Just like walking on the ground. I did that without even thinking about it.

The ledge was only a few feet wide, and the path spiraled steeply upward, but if you pressed your back against the cliff wall and kept your focus a few steps in front of you, you could almost forget how high you were climbing.

Almost.

We kept moving up and I glanced down from time to time, hoping to see Eric and Savannah far below us on the ground. Finally, we reached the peak of the outcrop. It was a tiny plateau, baked dry by the sun and barely big enough for the diamond-shaped footprint of the radio tower. Each metal strut was bolted deep into the ground, supported by a series of giant metal Xs crisscrossing up to the top, where a red beacon gleamed. Huge cables anchored into the support beams traversed down the sides of the cliff to help steady the tower. I looked to see where the other end of the cable went to, but the sight of the wire disappearing into the abyss made me dizzy.

At the base of one of the struts was the broadcast station, a tiny, windowless hut built of cinder blocks and painted the same color as the rocks. Set into the wall was a door.

Finally. I sprinted to the door and turned the handle.

Locked.

"Find a rock," I called to Howard. "A piece of metal. Something!" This was our last hope. Our only hope. We had to get a message out. "Check your pockets."

He did. "I've got a bottle of water and the code book. Actually, I'm pretty thirsty, so make that half a bottle of water."

I rolled my eyes and started searching my own pockets.

My Omega City flashlight, loaded with the Underberg battery, a bottle of water, and my cell phone. Which had . . .

"Howard," I breathed, as I stared down at the screen. "Look."

Reception.

TRUE BELIEVERS

DAD'S PHONE RANG SIX TIMES AND WENT TO VOICE MAIL. I TRIED AGAIN: voice mail.

"Leave a message," Howard said. "It's better than nothing."

I nodded.

"Dad, it's Gillian. We're on the island—the one in the middle of Eureka Cove. Dad, the Shepherds are here. We tried to call you but you didn't pick up. . . ."

I should have tried harder to convince him about the messages before he left us this morning. I should have called him the sixteenth time. I should have thought about this before jumping in.

"Anyway, we kayaked out here. They have these weird sheep experiments going on—we don't know what they are or why, but the sheep are really, really small and woolly. Um . . ."

I looked at Howard for help.

"Tell him about the space chimps."

"Oh yeah! There are these chimpanzees—"

The call waiting beeped in my ear. I checked the readout: Dad! I pressed the speakerphone.

"Dad! Are you okay?"

"Gillian?" His voice sounded worried. "Gillian, honey, where are you? We've been looking everywhere."

He was okay! I was torn between feeling relieved and wanting to blurt out everything we'd discovered.

"We're on the island, Dad!"

"I know," he said. "*Where* on the island? Half the Guidant security team is looking for you. They found your boats—"

Howard and I looked at each other, confused. "*Guidant* security? No, we only saw the Shepherds! Dad, the Shepherds are here! On the island!"

"Gillian?" A woman's voice broke in on the line. "It's Elana Mero. What are you doing out there? I know from your father's book that you make it a habit to go off exploring, but like I said, the island is abandoned. Everything there is falling to pieces. I would hate for you kids to get hurt—"

"It has *not* been abandoned!" I shouted into the phone. "You lied to us!"

"What? Just tell us where you are."

"Tell us what these chimps are doing out here!" I shot back.

"These what?" She sounded utterly baffled.

"*Chimpanzees.* Monkeys."

"Apes," Howard corrected.

"You have a whole geodesic dome full of monkeys and people are kidnapping them and doing experiments on them."

"And skeletons of the space chimps," Howard said. "Or at least, that's what they say they are."

"Yeah!" I added, though that seemed like a relatively minor crime.

For a second, there was silence on the line. "I have no idea what they're talking about, Sam. There's nothing out there but some broken-down buildings and a lot of weeds. Monkeys? That's ridiculous."

"Dad!" I cried. "Dad, listen to me." Not her. I'd seen the chimps with my own eyes.

"Gillian, tell us where you are," Dad said. "We'll send someone to pick you up."

"Not necessary, Sam," Elana interrupted again. "We

just tracked their signal. They're at the cell phone relay."

"It's a radio tower," I insisted.

"Gillian," Dad said sternly. "This isn't funny. You've caused a lot of trouble today. I had to call your mom to come back, she had to get Nate from his college tour . . . you just can't pull these kinds of stunts, kiddo. We're guests at Eureka Cove. Ms. Mero was very upset to learn that you'd wandered off the grid."

I gasped. Upset *we were off grid*? He'd practically invented the concept. What had happened to all his arguments about privacy and liberty? He didn't even sound like my father right now. "Dad, listen to yourself! We have every right not to be tracked."

"This isn't about freedom," he said. "It's about being safe."

"Quite right," said Elana in the background.

I stared down at the phone in disbelief. Then I did the only thing that made sense in that moment: I drew back my arm and tossed it off the cliff.

Howard watched the tiny silver box fly into the blue sky, then tumble down, down, down, and disappear.

"Well," said Howard. "That was interesting."

No, that was terrifying. My mind raced with possibilities. My father was brainwashed. Or he was being forced to say those things. Or maybe that wasn't Dad on the phone at all? Maybe she'd just . . . recorded his voice or something.

Could be anything.

"We have to get out of here," I said. "They're coming for us."

"Wasn't that the idea? That your dad would come and get us?"

"Not anymore!" I shouted. "Not when he's under the influence of Elana. Didn't you hear her? She's one of them!"

Howard was silent, considering this; then he reached up and unzipped his hood. He stood there, staring down for a second, then lifted his head and looked me in the eye.

"Gillian, you're very smart, and I tend to think that you know what you're doing. But Eric and Savannah aren't here right now, and they're the ones who usually tell you when you're acting crazy. So I have to." He took a deep breath. "Throwing away that phone was really crazy."

"They were using it to track us!"

"So? You told them where we were already. And we could have used the phone to call your mother. Or my mother. Or Nate."

The afternoon sun beat down on our heads, but beneath the neckline of my utility suit, cooling setting three, I hardly felt it. Still, I was burning up inside.

"And what if Elana Mero is telling the truth?" he went on. "Maybe she believes what she's telling us—that the messages are a school project, that the island is abandoned and in ruins . . . she has a big international company to run.

How would she know what's happening on every square inch of this campus?"

But nothing else added up, most of all Dad. "These experiments didn't just spring up out of nowhere, and it couldn't have happened behind her back. You saw that chimp habitat! You think they built that place for an agricultural experiment? Those alcoves, those skeletons, those plaques?"

Howard's forehead furrowed. "Right."

"I know it doesn't make sense. None of this makes sense. Why would she have us here if she was a Shepherd? Why would she offer Dad a job, or promote his book about Omega City?" I shook my face and gestured to the complex below us. "But look at this place. It's crawling with Shepherds. It's *impossible* that she doesn't know."

"Okay . . ." Howard thought about this. "So she's lying."

"Yes," I said. "Like Fiona." Except that didn't feel right at all, and judging by the look on Howard's face, he knew it, too.

"Or maybe it's someone else at Guidant," he said. "Someone high up enough to get all this stuff done without the boss knowing."

"Like who?"

Just then, we heard a sound from the broadcast station hut. We turned just in time to see the door open. The person inside took two steps into the sunlight and stopped dead as she saw us.

Black pants, black boots, and a jacket emblazoned with the Shepherd symbol, but the first thing I noticed was her pretty, sculpted bronze hair. Dani Alcestis. And she was a Shepherd.

The expression on her face was one of shock as she looked from me to Howard. "How did you get up here? How—how did you get here at all?"

Howard stepped closer to me, even as I was flooded with relief. Dani clearly hadn't expected to see us here, which meant her boss hadn't sent her. Which meant maybe Elana Mero was telling the truth. That my dad was safe.

Meanwhile, we were in real trouble.

"You kids need to leave, right now." Her face was full of fear. That faker.

What a perfect cover! As Elana's assistant, Dani had access to all kinds of resources, and she could easily hide the truth from the rest of the company.

"Don't worry," I snapped. "Your boss is sending someone for us."

"You called Elana?" Dani asked, frantic. "From here? What did you tell her?"

"Everything!" Howard broke in. "About the sheep and the chimps and everything."

She rolled her eyes and snorted. "Oh, so that's everything, huh? *Idiots.* I told him you were idiots."

"Told who? My dad?" I asked, confused.

Dani just shook her head in disgust. "And now you've ruined our last chance."

"Good!" I cried. "You have a bunch of scared chimpanzees in a lab made of broken glass. Whatever you're doing here deserves to get ruined."

"You're right about that," she shot back. "But no matter what you think you discovered, you haven't even scratched the surface of what is going on here, and it's way too late to explain it all now."

"Why, because of phase two?"

That got her attention. She glared at me. "What do you know?"

"Oh, so we're not idiots anymore?" I scoffed. "We know the numbers station isn't a school project like you told Elana it was. We broke your stupid code."

Now she really looked scared. "What do you mean, you broke it?"

"It wasn't that hard," said Howard. "Not with Dr. Underberg's book."

Dani trained her laser focus on him. "What's this about Dr. Underberg?"

"He gave me a book on how to break number ciphers."

"He did what?" she asked, furious.

"And we used it to figure out your Shepherd messages," I broke in.

Dani looked from me to Howard and back again, a strange, puzzled look on her face. "Wait. Shepherd messages?"

"Yes," I shouted triumphantly. "And we told Dad and Elana exactly what they said."

Dani's whole demeanor changed. She jerked backward, and her mouth snapped shut as she seemed to come to some sudden realization. "You told . . . you told Elana Mero what my messages said?"

"You'll never get away with it now!"

Dani snorted. "Yes, you've made that nearly impossible. *Brilliant* job," she said, sarcastic. She looked up at the blue sky. "What in the world am I supposed to do now?"

The sky didn't answer, but I did.

"Elana said she and my dad were coming to get us."

"Elana is coming here?" She stared down her nose at me. "Kid, if I were you, I'd run. Far."

Before we could respond, Dani took off, sprinting at full speed toward the edge of the cliff. When she reached the end she leaped out over the void, ducking her head between outstretched arms. Howard and I hurried after her, only to see her drop like a diving bird toward the water far below. My breath seemed to catch in my throat as she fell, a dark spot against the bright waves, and then she vanished beneath the surface with a smooth, tiny splash. We waited for her to bob back up, but there was no sign.

"Whoa," I said.

"Yeah." Howard blinked. "That has to be more than a hundred feet. She must be trained. Or dead."

She'd kept her form the whole way down. I doubted she was dead.

"I've never seen anyone do that for real," Howard went on. "Eric will be so mad he missed it."

Eric's disappointment at not seeing death-defying acts of cliff diving was the least of my concerns. "Where did she go? She has to come up sometime, right?"

Another ten seconds passed, but there was no sign of her in the water. The last thing I ever expected was to be caught by a Shepherd . . . who then ran away.

But at least we had one question answered. "You were right, Howard. It *is* someone close to Ms. Mero." As Elana's assistant, Dani would have complete control over what information reached her boss's ears. She'd also be able to issue orders in Elana's name. She could find a way to sneak all kinds of Shepherd equipment to this supposedly "abandoned" island without anyone being the wiser.

"Who is 'him'?" Howard asked. "Miss Alcestis said she told 'him' we were idiots. But she couldn't have been talking about Dr. Seagret."

"It must be Anton Everett," I replied. "You heard him at dinner last night. And he's a vice president at Guidant. If he's a Shepherd, too, it makes sense that he could run experiments here behind Elana's back. He could have been the one to build the geodesic dome for the chimps. He could have been the one to—"

"Steal the space chimps and their remains," Howard finished. "I can't believe everything I've read about them—about what happened to them—was a lie. Instead they were trapped here, subject to more experiments. . . ."

"Yeah." More lies.

"I hope Savannah's wrong, and there's something we can do to help them."

"My dad will know." That is, if Dad ever spoke to me again after everything I'd put him through today. One thing was for sure, I was in big trouble for tossing my cell phone. I didn't know how I planned to explain that one.

Sorry, Dad, but when you started freaking out about us not being trackable by cell phone and saying it was better for us to be safe than to be free, I thought you'd been kidnapped and brainwashed by Them.

"Let's find Eric and Savannah," I said. "You look for them down that side and I'll look over here, in case they turned around at the cliff and headed in our direction."

I scanned the ground beneath us for the telltale glint of their Omega City utility suits, feeling even more stupid as I did. They might be invisible to infrared cameras, but shiny silver suits stuck out like a sore thumb against green underbrush and brown rocks. The Shepherds would be able to spot us a mile away.

"Gillian!" Howard called from behind me.

"Did you find them?" I turned around, but Howard wasn't on the other side of the peak. Instead, he was inside the tiny broadcasting station. I followed him inside the dingy cinder-block hut. There wasn't much to see: a folding chair and card table topped by a radio, a microphone, and a set of headphones. No wonder Dani hadn't been able to hear us at the door.

"You're supposed to be looking for the others."

"Check this out." He handed me a stack of papers covered with the familiar-looking square code charts we'd spent the last two days working on. "These are all the messages. Look, here are the ones we decoded yesterday." He handed me encryption sheets for "Mary Had a Little Lamb" and "Baa, Baa, Black Sheep." "And here are a few more. I was right, by the way. The key is always the first five-letter word with no repeating letters in the rhyme."

I examined the papers. Next to the codes we'd already broken were several more. Well, that at least solved the mystery of the messages. They were being broadcast from here, and the woman's voice? It was Dani all along.

One code was for "Little Bo Peep."

	1	*2*	*3*	*4*	*5*
1	*A*	*L*	*O*	*N*	*E*
2	*B*	*C*	*D*	*F*	*G*
3	*H*	*I*	*J*	*K*	*M*
4	*P*	*Q*	*R*	*S*	*T*
5	*U*	*V*	*W*	*Y*	*X/Z*

44 15 11 25 43 15 45 44 11 22 22

S E A G R E T S A C C

15 41 45 15 23 32 14 52 32 45 11

E P T E D I N V I T A

45 32 13 14 45 13 44 41 15 11 34

T I O N T O S P E A K

11 45 25 51 32 23 11 14 45 41 12

A T G U I D A N T P L

15 11 44 15 11 23 52 32 44 15

E A S E A D V I S E

Seagrets accepted invitation to speak at Guidant. Please advise.

At the sight of our name on this message, my blood ran cold. The Shepherds had known we were coming the whole time. All this time, I'd been so excited to come with Dad to Guidant, and I'd been leading us right to his worst enemy.

Another was for "Little Boy Blue."

	1	*2*	*3*	*4*	*5*
1	*A*	*F*	*T*	*E*	*R*
2	*B*	*C*	*D*	*G*	*H*
3	*I*	*J*	*K*	*L*	*M*
4	*N*	*O*	*P*	*Q*	*S*
5	*U*	*V*	*W*	*Y*	*X/Z*

41 14 14 23 22 42 41 12 31 15
N E E D C O N F I R

35 11 13 31 42 41 42 12 22 11
M A T I O N O F C A

43 14 34 34 11 23 11 13 11 13
P E L L A D A T A T

11 35 43 14 15 31 41 24 14 55
A M P E R I N G E X

43	14	22	13	22	42	51	41	13	14
P	*E*	*C*	*T*	*C*	*O*	*U*	*N*	*T*	*E*

15	11	13	13	11	22	33
R	*A*	*T*	*T*	*A*	*C*	*K*

Need confirmation of Capella data tampering. Expect counterattack.

I frowned. "Capella . . . that's the satellite program we saw today. The one looking for near-Earth asteroids."

"Yes." Howard nodded.

"Why would the Shepherds tamper with the data? Wouldn't that put us in danger?"

"If there was an asteroid coming and they made it look like there wasn't, yeah, it would." Howard said.

"Well, of course!" I cried. "What else would they do?"

Howard shrugged. "The other thing. If an asteroid *wasn't* coming and they made it look like there was."

I rolled my eyes. "Who would do that, pretend like an asteroid was going to hit the Earth?"

He rolled his eyes, too, but on him it looked ridiculous. "Gee, Gillian, isn't that what you think the aliens or the Russian military or whatever did at Tunguska? Blow something up and then pretend it was just an airburst as a cover-up?"

I thought about that for a moment. "You're right.

But why would the Shepherds want to do that? Dad said they wanted to lead us, to help us survive. Like building Omega City with Dr. Underberg."

"Yeah," said Howard. "But Omega City is gone. And if the Earth was destroyed by an asteroid, Omega City wouldn't be much use, anyway. It's like Anton said last night—we should have colonies on Mars."

"Howard! Of course!"

"What?"

"If you thought an asteroid was going to destroy the Earth, what is the first thing you'd wish for?"

"That I'd gone up in that rocket with Dr. Underberg when I had the chance."

"Yes, exactly."

Howard looked at me, expectant. "I want that anyway."

"Well, if an asteroid really was coming, the whole world would agree with you. We'd *all* want to get off the planet."

"And go where?" Howard asked. "There's not much room on the International Space Station."

"Right. There's not much room anywhere . . . yet." That's exactly what Anton and Dani had been saying at dinner last night. That there was nothing protecting humanity, should a big rock from outer space try to smash us into smithereens.

"What about this last one?" Howard asked, showing

me the final sheet, which went to something called "Tender Shepherd."

	1	*2*	*3*	*4*	*5*
1	*C*	*O*	*U*	*N*	*T*
2	*A*	*B*	*D*	*E*	*F*
3	*G*	*H*	*I*	*J*	*K*
4	*L*	*M*	*P*	*Q*	*R*
5	*S*	*V*	*W*	*Y*	*X/Z*

33	*14*	*25*	*33*	*14*	*33*	*15*	*54*	*22*	*21*	*51*
I	*N*	*F*	*I*	*N*	*I*	*T*	*Y*	*B*	*A*	*S*
24	*33*	*51*	*14*	*12*	*15*	*51*	*24*	*11*	*13*	*45*
E	*I*	*S*	*N*	*O*	*T*	*S*	*E*	*C*	*U*	*R*
24	*43*	*45*	*24*	*43*	*21*	*45*	*24*	*25*	*12*	*45*
E	*P*	*R*	*E*	*P*	*A*	*R*	*E*	*F*	*O*	*R*
24	*52*	*21*	*11*	*13*	*21*	*15*	*33*	*12*	*14*	
E	*V*	*A*	*C*	*U*	*A*	*T*	*I*	*O*	*N*	

Infinity Base is not secure. Prepare for evacuation.

"What's Infinity Base?" Howard asked. "The island?"

"I guess so. Or some other Shepherd base." Honestly,

I hadn't a clue. "Take all of it. The more evidence we have of the Shepherds' work, the better." Hopefully Dad could figure out what these mysterious phrases meant, or what the Shepherds were even doing here.

Or why they cared so much about us.

We left the station and made another circuit around the perimeter of the peak, searching for Eric and Savannah. Finally, close to one of the metal struts of the tower, we saw them scrambling over the rocks at the base of the cliff.

"Savannah!" I shouted. The tiny figures paused and turned in circles as if seeking the origin of the noise. "Up here!"

They looked up for a moment, and then they turned and ran.

A few seconds later, I saw why, as several guards swarmed over the boulders in pursuit.

Howard and I shrank back from the edge. I clutched his arm. "Oh, no. The Shepherds found them."

Wait. Technically, they'd found us, too. At least, Dani had. And she'd been the one to run away.

I hoped that was a good thing. It meant Dani was afraid of Elana. If we could hold out until Elana and Dad sent someone to fetch us, maybe we could still stop . . . well, whatever phase two and all the rest of this stuff was.

I bit my lip, watching helplessly as the tiny silver figures darted across the landscape, chased by the guards in black.

This was awful. Back in Omega City, I'd been forced to sit and listen to Eric and my friends crawling through the air tunnels as they were chased by Fiona's goons. And now there was nothing I could do from all the way up here but hope for the best.

All of a sudden, we lost sight of them.

"I think they went into that building down there," Howard said, pointing at one of the three vine-covered outer buildings near the sheep paddocks. "At least, I think they did. But the Shepherds went into the woods. I think they lost them."

"We have to get down there."

"And get captured, too?"

"We're no safer up here," I pointed out. "And Elana is sending help. If we get to Eric and Sav, at least we'll all be together when help comes."

"Right." Howard went over to one of the support wires stretched between the base of the cliffs and the tower struts and plucked it. "Seems secure."

"What do you mean?" I took two steps back.

He shrugged and started digging in his pockets. "Do you know how long it will take us to reach them if we go back down the path?"

I shook my head as my throat closed up. "No. No way. You want us to climb down the wire?" My voice was shrill.

He pulled out a couple of metal climbing hooks. "No. Not climb. Slide. We'll use these carabiners to make a zip line."

I let out a squeak of pure terror.

"Come on, Gillian." He threaded one of the carabiners through his utility-suit belt. "My brother taught me how."

No way. Also, what else did he have in his pockets? The code book, carabiners . . . Didn't it all get heavy?

"This is just like the grappling hooks," he went on, "but in reverse."

"The grappling hooks were a matter of life or death," I whispered hoarsely. My voice was no longer working. "We were escaping an exploding rocket ship."

Howard hooked his belt carabiner onto the wire. "Okay. Pretend there's a rocket ship exploding behind you."

I shook my head wildly.

He frowned. "I'll help." He leaned in, eyes wide. "Boom. Boom."

He sounded so ridiculous that I couldn't help it. I covered my mouth with my hands and giggled.

Howard hooked the other carabiner onto my belt.

"No," I cried as Howard secured our belts to each other with the carabiner. I reeled back. "No, no, Howard, I can't."

He grabbed me in a bear hug. "Here we go. Don't scream."

I couldn't make promises, though I knew that might bring the Shepherds running.

"Oh, and better tuck back your braid."

I gulped and shoved the end of my hair deep inside my suit. "How are we going to brake at the bottom?"

"We'll use our feet."

"We'll break our legs!"

"Hmm." Howard pulled off his sneakers and fitted them over his hands. "Okay, let's try this. Hold on tight."

Try? I clung to Howard for dear life, and he pushed us off the edge of the cliff.

CREEPY CRAWLERS

Don't scream, don't scream, don't scream.

Even though we were attached to the wire with carabiners, it still felt like free fall. Wind whooshed by my ears, and I ducked my head into the zippered collar of my utility suit, barely registering the scenery as it grew larger and larger beneath us. I could hear Howard's labored breathing as he fought to keep hold of the wire between his sneaker soles. The smell of burnt rubber stung my nostrils, and I wondered what would happen if the friction burned through his sneakers entirely.

"Brace yourself!" Howard called.

I dared to look. We were about thirty feet off the ground and falling fast.

"Howard! Brake!"

"I'm trying," he gasped. But it wasn't enough.

We flew through the air and the ground rushed up to meet us. I was too frightened to scream. We were going to crash!

Desperately, I swung my legs up and hooked my legs around the wire, bracing myself for the stinging bite as the metal cut through the thin silver material of my suit.

A humming, metallic zing filled my ears as the suit rubbed the wires, but we slowed. A second later, we hit the ground hard, tumbling to a heap on the rocky surface at the base of the outcrop.

"Uff!" I grunted from underneath Howard. "Get up!"

"I'm getting us unhooked."

"Up!" I moaned, and shoved at him. "We have to hide in case anyone saw us on the zip line."

We disentangled ourselves from the wire, and Howard shoved his feet back into his sneakers. The soles were completely rubbed through in the center. I checked out the backs of the knees on my utility suit. Where the wire had rubbed against them, the silver was even brighter, and hot to the touch, but otherwise undamaged.

"Wow," I said. "Someday, we're going to have to find

out what this stuff is made of."

"I've been trying all summer," Howard said. "I know you and your dad are fans of the battery, but I can't wait until they start making this suit."

I stared up at the outcrop, marveling at how far we'd come in seconds. It wasn't flying up through the fiery depths of a rocket-ship silo, but it was still quite the ride.

Now that we were down on the ground, I felt disoriented. Which building was the one we'd seen Eric and Savannah disappear into? They all looked the same—boxy slabs of concrete overgrown with tangled green vines. I didn't even see doors on them.

"Come on." I urged Howard forward. "Let's get out of here before the Shepherds find us."

I started off, but Howard stopped me. "They went that way." He pointed to the right-most building, and together, we headed in that direction.

Even up close, where the dull walls were visible beneath the matted ivy leaves, it looked impenetrable. Why would someone make a building with no windows and no doors? I thought about the drones that had fed the sheep. "What if the entrances are on the roof? For drones or helicopters or something?"

Howard looked up the sides. "I'm not climbing this ivy."

Me neither. I might smell like a chimpanzee, but that

was as far as it went. Still, Eric and Savannah had gone somewhere. We started circling the building, looking to see if there was a door or window we'd missed.

"Gills," said Eric's voice. I spun around, but saw nothing.

"Did you hear that?" I asked Howard.

"Gills!" Eric cried again. "Watch out!"

The last thing I saw as the greenery beneath my feet gave way was a pair of hands shooting up through the leaves.

I dropped through the ground in a tangle of dead leaves and dust. Twigs scratched the bare skin of my face and vines snagged on my arms and legs. I twisted and writhed, fighting against the vines and the hands reaching out of them.

"Let go!" I cried, swinging wildly at whatever had me in its grip. *"Let me go!"*

I fell hard onto a debris-ridden concrete floor about four feet below the surface.

"Geez, Gills, try not to knock out my fake teeth, too." Eric pulled back, brushing bits of vine off his arms, and I realized he'd only been trying to break my fall.

I stood, shaking my head and looking through the shadows at the dusty faces of Eric and Savannah, who was sitting with her back to one of the far walls, a sheaf of paper on her lap. We were alone in a small, concrete depression in the earth. To one side was a narrow band of windows leading into the basement of the nearby building. This well must have been built to allow light into the basement. A rusty ladder led down from one of the concrete walls, and the entire surface above our head was covered with a carpet of vines.

"Gillian?" Howard crouched over the hole I'd just made in the overgrowth. "Hey. What are you all doing down there?"

"Hiding," said Eric.

"Howard!" Savannah beckoned to him. "Get down here quick, and let's get covered up again."

Howard hopped down beside us, and Savannah and Eric worked to prop up the edges of the vines to make the space look undisturbed.

"Where are we?" I whispered.

"Safe," said Savannah. "Or *safer*, at least. Were you guys chased, too?"

"No," I said. "In fact, it was kind of the opposite." Quickly, I explained what had happened up at the tower.

"So Dani was the one sending those messages?" Savannah blinked incredulously at me. "Do you think she's the one running the show here?"

"Her," I said, "or Anton. Maybe when Elana decided to move Guidant off the island, he moved the Shepherds in."

"And you think Anton has the Shepherds tampering

with the Capella data to make it look like an asteroid is going to hit the Earth?"

"You heard him at dinner!" I exclaimed. "All that stuff about how we need backup colonies of humans all over the solar system in case the world gets destroyed."

"Hmm," Savannah said. "But he also said we *don't* have colonies and stuff. It's not like he can say we're going to get hit by an asteroid, and so we all pack up and move to Mars tomorrow."

"Well the other option is we *are* going to get hit by an asteroid, and he's hiding the data that warns us."

We all looked up through the vines at the sky. I hoped that wasn't the case, either.

"I want to hear more about how Dad called Mom and told her to get back here," Eric said. "Maybe she can stop this flood of crazy that's happening."

"Oh, I told Gillian she was acting crazy," said Howard. "Back when she said Elana was a Shepherd."

"And I am on your side now," I replied. "We caught Dani red-handed."

"Dani," echoed Savannah. "Elana's *assistant.*"

"Believe me, she's not a huge fan of her boss," I said. "She jumped off a cliff when we said we'd called Elana and she was coming to get us."

"Yeah, and she said we should run, too," Howard added.

"Run?" Savannah asked. "From Elana?" She looked pensive.

"What?" I asked her.

"I was just thinking about how the only people Fiona was afraid of were the Shepherds. She told you to be afraid of them, too."

"Well, I am afraid. And Dani is a Shepherd."

"So then, what does it say that *Dani* is afraid of Elana?"

"It says she's her boss," Eric cut in. "And that the Shepherds won't stop Elana when she comes to rescue us. Come on, Sav. Don't encourage her."

I looked from Savannah to Eric. "What is that supposed to mean?" I stood up and put my hands on my hips. "You all think I'm crazy?"

"No," said Eric. "We're here, aren't we?" He seemed to regret those words the second they left his mouth. His face changed completely. "That's not what I meant."

"Of course it is." Mom left Dad because she thought he was crazy, too. Maybe she'd think Eric and I were crazy now. "Don't worry about what Mom will say when we see her. You can tell her this was all my idea."

"Gills . . ."

The leaves over our head began to shake; then the ground began to rumble. We crouched, clinging to one another, as the shaking grew stronger and stronger, then faded away.

"What *is* that?" I asked. It was the same thing that had happened at the chimp habitat.

"The launch of phase two?" Eric suggested. "It happens every thirty minutes or so."

"They aren't launching anything," said Howard. "We would have seen it from on top of the cliff."

"We didn't see anything, but trust me, you can feel the rumbling from the ground," Eric said.

"Have you been chased the whole time?" I asked.

"No," said Savannah. "But this hiding spot is better than the last one."

"Yeah," said Eric. "Savannah's practically made it her office. She's been *reading*."

"I just want to know what's going on with those chimps."

So did I. I drew closer.

Savannah wrinkled her nose and scooted away from me. "I notice you didn't stop to dunk your head."

"It wasn't like there was a bathroom up there on the cliff. Or anywhere else."

"Tell me about it," Sav said. "Your brother used a tree."

I peered into the windows against the building's wall, but the interior was too dark to see anything. "Think there are bathrooms in here?"

"It's worth a shot. Whatever they have has got to be better than a tree."

I ran my fingers along the window frame. "Could we kick it in?"

"Let's try." Eric lay down on his back with his feet across from a window. "Help me. On three."

I lay down beside him and drew my legs back.

"One," I said.

"Two," he added.

"Three!" We kicked out.

The windowpane popped free from the frame, and a second later, I heard it shatter against the floor in the room below.

Eric stuck his head through the hole. "Some kind of basement. This window's up near the ceiling, but we can lower ourselves down."

"Can you see anything?" I asked.

"Desks." He shrugged. "A few computer terminals. Looks abandoned, like everything else around here."

"Well, maybe they left the water on," I said. "Let's check it out." Carefully, Eric and I lowered ourselves, feet first, into the room. My feet scrabbled against the side of the wall as I reached tentatively out with my toes for a ledge or a shelf or a tabletop, but I felt nothing.

"I can't hold on," I said in a huff as the corner of the ledge dug into my armpits. "Eric?"

"Got it," his voice floated up beside me. He'd lowered

himself all the way down, and was hanging by his fingertips. "Just a second." He let go of the ledge and slipped down the wall. There was a huge crash.

"Eric!" I screamed, hanging from my arms on the ledge, my feet wheeling out into darkness.

"I'm okay," he called from below. "I just . . . flipped the table or whatever I was standing on. It's fine. Just drop."

I did as he said, landing hard on the floor several feet down. Something crunched and crackled beneath the soles of my feet.

The dark room smelled stale and brown, like a root cellar or an old shed. The dim light from the window wasn't enough to illuminate anything, and got even dimmer as the shapes of Savannah and Howard blocked the window as they followed us. I stepped away from the wall to let them drop, and kicked something on the crackly ground. It skittered away from me.

Savannah and Howard crunched down behind me as I brushed debris off my pocket and reached inside for my flashlight. Time to see what was going on in here.

I flicked the switch. The beam caught the white glow of a skull, lying an inch deep in a brown, wriggling mass on the floor.

Wriggling . . .

I raised the flashlight to my brother. His feet, his legs,

his entire body was crawling with—bugs.

Shiny, crackly-carapaced, six-legged beetles crawled everywhere. The floors, the walls, the tipped-over legs and broken edges of the aquarium table we'd upended, and, worst of all, the glimmering silver material of Eric's utility suit. There must be hundreds of them. Thousands.

I dropped the flashlight and clapped a hand over my mouth to stifle my own scream. There was nothing, *nothing* my brother hated more than bugs. The beam of light washed weakly over the walls.

"What is it?" Eric swiped at his face and the beetles went flying. "What?"

I reached for my flashlight, and a beetle crawled over it. I grimaced as its stubby little antennae waved across the beam. The shadow of a giant bug head graced the wall.

"Um, Eric," I said gently, kicking the flashlight to dislodge the bug. "Don't freak out, but—"

Howard flipped on the lights, bathing the room in a wan fluorescent glow. Giant aquarium tanks lined the walls, and inside each lay fresh white bones and thousands upon thousands of brown-black beetles. Savannah and I shied away from the bugs spreading like a puddle across the floor. Eric was positively covered in them.

He looked down at his body, let out a high-pitched squeal, and started jumping up and down. "Get them off! Get them off, getthemoff, *getthemoff!*"

He batted at his legs and shrieked. "Gillian! Help me!"

"Hold on!" I started swiping at his clothes. "Eric, hold still!"

"I can't! I can't!" He danced from side to side, pumping his legs like a giant silver grasshopper, which only made him lose his footing and fall back among the beetles. He tried to turn over, smacked into bare skull, and went completely berserk as the beetles swarmed his arms.

Savannah threw back her head and laughed.

"Sav!" I hissed as I knelt among the crunching black carapaces and swatted bugs off my brother. "Not funny! He's going to get eaten alive!"

"Nah," she said, and kicked waves of the bugs away with her feet. "Those are dermestids."

"Derma-what?"

"Dermestid beetles. Oh, you are *so* not country, Gillian."

I paused in my frantic attempts to delouse Eric. Horseflies I knew, and carpenter ants. What was an especially backwoods bug?

Howard came forward with a broom, sweeping a clear path among the insects. He started brushing them off Eric. The broom worked way better than my hands. "They use them in taxidermy. My dad has a colony. They're flesh eaters."

Eric whimpered.

"*Dead* flesh," Savannah clarified. "They're super gross, but they don't bite humans."

Eric shot to his feet and shook out his hair. "Are there any down the back of my suit?" He shuddered. "Help me. Help me!"

I double-checked for stragglers on my brother while Howard swept the bugs back into the remains of the broken aquarium, and Savannah examined the other tanks.

"These look like more chimpanzee skeletons," she said sadly.

"They gave the chimps to the bugs to eat?" I asked, horrified.

"They gave *corpses* to the bugs," Sav said. "Dermestid beetles only eat dead things, remember? That's what makes them so great for taxidermists trying to get skeletons. They'll clean a skull in no time, and it's much easier and you get way better results than trying to do it yourself, or using chemicals. All the hunters in town—even Mr. Noland—keep a tank or two in their workshop for when they clean deer carcasses for stuffing."

"You people have these things in your basements?"

"Not me," said Savannah. "I don't have a basement. And Mom doesn't hunt, anyway."

"Museums use them, too," Howard added. "It's not weird or anything."

"Um, yes it is!" insisted Eric. "It's super weird."

I nodded in agreement. There was no way museums used bugs to clean off specimens. And I bet Savannah wouldn't be so calm if they'd been crawling all over her!

"Your dad keeps maps of Area fifty-one," Savannah shot back. "At least these bugs are real."

Eric was too scared to argue. "Can we please go now?" he begged, his eyes wide.

Sav had her hand pressed against another tank. "Look, this one was a juvenile," she said.

I made the mistake of glancing inside. An even smaller, more childlike skeleton was nestled among the crawling beetles. "This is disgusting."

"I wish I knew why they were doing it," Savannah said softly. She shook her head. "Those beautiful creatures!"

"Please tell me she's not talking about the bugs." Eric had his back flattened to the wall farthest from the tanks. "Let's get out of here. Come on. What are we waiting for?"

"But where is here?" I asked. "Let's figure out a plan. We have to hide from the Shepherds until Elana and Dad come."

"Do we know where they're meeting us?" Savannah asked.

I looked at Howard, who stared at the floor and shrugged.

"We . . . kinda didn't finish the conversation with them."

Eric and Savannah turned to me.

"I . . . um, might have thrown the phone off a cliff."

"Oh, Gills . . ." Eric let his head thump against the wall. He looked pale. "What, did they threaten to put Mom on the phone?"

"Hey!" Savannah and I cried.

"It's true!" Eric said, indignant. "She shuts down the second Mom tries to do anything with her. She has all summer!"

"That's hardly important now," Savannah said. I loved her for sticking up for me, but it didn't stop the lump in my throat.

I stared down at my hands. "It wasn't Mom," I said softly. "It . . . it was Dad."

"What was Dad?" Eric leaned forward.

"He didn't sound like himself," I said. "He was talking about how angry he was that I'd gone off grid, and how it was okay for us to sacrifice our freedom for safety."

"You mean he sounded like a normal person for a change?" Eric said.

"You're right," I snapped. "Dad's *not normal.* He doesn't think like normal people, like *Mom.* But that's what I mean. He sounded different. And I didn't like it."

"*I'd* like it," Eric said. "I actually really liked it this summer, knowing that dinner wouldn't poison me and the house wasn't going to burn down every night. I liked that

Mom was there with clean laundry and to take me to swim practice. If Dad was like that all the time, I wouldn't want to go to Idaho, either."

I crossed my arms over my chest. "If Dad were like that all the time, no one would be going to Idaho, because—" My jaw snapped shut.

It was so silent in the room you could almost hear the crunch of thousands of dermestid mandibles ripping apart thousands of scraps of dead meat.

If Dad were like that all the time, he and Mom would not be divorced. He'd still be at the university. We'd still be a family, and Omega City would be nothing but a myth.

I drew in a single, shaking breath. "We'll go back to the beach," I said with finality. "They can't miss us there."

Savannah took the cue. "Great. But you, Gillian, are finding a bathroom first. We need to wash that poop out of your hair."

18

SWEET DREAMS

LUCKILY, THERE WAS A BATHROOM DOWN THE HALL FROM THE DERMES-tid beetle room. Savannah and I made use of their hand soap, and Eric stripped nearly naked under the air dryers, hoping to blow every last remnant of the beetles off him.

"You're lucky we're underground," Howard said, as he helped my brother aim the nozzle of the air dryer on every nook and cranny. "Above eighty degrees, dermestids can fly."

Eric looked faint.

Savannah, meanwhile, was scrubbing my scalp under the faucet. "I still want to know what they're doing with those apes." She started rinsing out my hair. "All those skeletons."

"Ow." I pulled my head out. "I want some hair left."

"Sorry." She held up sudsy hands. "This soap isn't exactly tangle free."

"I was much more gentle on your hair last night." I wrapped my head in a pile of paper towels. It might not have been fine shampoo, but I had to admit my hair smelled much nicer than it had all afternoon. "What did the papers from the chimp habitat say?"

"Not a lot that made sense," Savannah said. "There were a bunch of different tests. Bone density and muscle loss and stuff, and then there was another set where they were giving the chimps the same intelligence tests, over and over and over. Do you want to see?" She unzipped her pocket and pulled out the paperwork.

"Orbital duration," I read aloud, then turned to Howard, who was studying the codes we'd found at the radio station. "Orbital. Does that sound like they put the chimps in space?"

"Yes," he said without looking up. "If they mean the time they spent in orbit. Especially since it's a bone density test. Space travel is known for destroying bone density and muscle mass, because of the lack of gravity. That's why they make the astronauts on the space station work out on treadmills and stuff."

I considered this. So they put the chimps in space, then bred them, then put *those* chimps in space, and bred *them*. . . .

I thought about the skeletons. And then they killed them and let the beetles clean their bones, and tested their bone density. . . .

Back at the beginning of the space program, NASA had studied the chimps, too. They wanted to make sure apes could survive in space before they sent up humans. What if the Shepherds were doing the same thing?

"They want to know if we could survive in space for generations," I said. "They're breeding the chimps and testing them to see if we can make it as a species if we have to go to space. Permanently."

"But where are they putting these chimps, up in space?" Savannah asked. She was sitting on the edge of the counter, zipping and unzipping the neck of her utility suit. "They don't have a space station."

"I don't know." I said. "But it's like Anton said at dinner about focusing on space exploration. Clearly the Shepherds think our next step is living in space."

"Can we figure this stuff out after we get rescued?" Eric asked. "It shouldn't take too long for Elana and Dad to get out to the island. They could already be here."

"True. They aren't going to find us in an underground bathroom. Let's look for a way out."

"A way that doesn't involve going back to the dermestid room," Eric added.

We got ourselves together and took off down the hall. Despite the size of the building, there were only three more rooms on this floor. One was clearly just storage, and another, marked *Lady Birds,* looked empty when we peeked through the small window set into the door.

"Figures," said Eric. "If it's birds."

Savannah laughed. "No, it's a misspelling. Ladybirds is another name for ladybugs."

"Oh," said Eric. "Well, that's not too bad." But I noticed he still shuddered and swatted nervously at the back of his neck.

Near the end of the hall, we passed a door marked *Sericulture.*

I directed my flashlight inside. Giant webs crisscrossed the space, spilling out from the boxes that lined the walls. Soft, dark shapes fluttered about and twitched in the dim light from the high windows, caught in webs of their own making.

"Eww," said Eric. "Spiders."

"Those look like moths," said Howard.

Multiple signs posted on the door featured the Shepherd symbols and the animals' stats in simple black and white. Most of the signs had "completion dates" marked on them, but two did not:

GROUP 5

SILK PRODUCTION: SATISFACTORY
SILK STRENGTH: IDEAL
JAM PRODUCTION: UNSATISFACTORY
REPRODUCTION RATING: IDEAL
RESOURCE RATING: SATISFACTORY
COMPLETION DATE:

GROUP 17

SILK PRODUCTION: SATISFACTORY
SILK STRENGTH: UNSATISFACTORY
JAM PRODUCTION: IDEAL
REPRODUCTION RATING: SATISFACTORY
RESOURCE RATING: SATISFACTORY
COMPLETION DATE:

"Silk production . . . do you think these are silkworms?"

"Don't open the door and find out!" Eric begged. "Come on, we have to hurry and meet Dad."

"Right," I said, still staring at the moths. "But the more info we have for him, the better, right?"

"No," said Eric. "Not when it's bugs."

"They look like moths to me," said Howard.

"Silkworms aren't worms," said Savannah. "They're caterpillars. So maybe the moths are the adults. What do you think they mean by 'jam'?"

"You can eat moths," Howard said.

"No." Eric's tone was final.

"Yes," Howard said. "You crush them into a paste, like peanut butter. It's a great source of protein. They've looked into it for astronauts, but they'd have to eat, like, two hundred moths a day."

Savannah and I gagged. Eric, I think, might have actually thrown up a little in his mouth. *Moth* jam?

But once I got past the gross-out factor, another thought occurred to me. First the Shepherds had a bunch of space chimps, and now they were rating possible astronaut food. Was this entire island filled with projects to help humanity make it in space? After all, in a space station, there wasn't room for cotton fields. We'd have to make our clothes out of silk, or . . .

"Wool," I blurted. "Wool, and meat. Silk and jam."

"Peas and carrots," said Eric. "What's your point?"

"Those tiny sheep. They wouldn't take up much room on a spaceship."

"Yeah," said Eric, "but do you know how much sheep fart?"

I ignored him, but Howard didn't.

"They were measuring how much they fart, actually," said Howard. "They were keeping data on the methane production."

"Eww!" I cried, even though that probably was important. You wouldn't want to live on a spaceship full of sheep farts. It still fit my theory. "And they can be used to provide cloth and meat, which makes them doubly useful. And then these worms, they can fit into an even smaller space. . . ."

"And you can eat them, too!" said Howard.

"I'd rather get hit by an asteroid," said Eric.

I examined the listings again. As with the flocks of sheep, the groups whose "resource rating" was listed as satisfactory showed no "completion date." They must be the successful experiments. I thought about the mama chimp the Shepherds had captured. Would her experiment be successful, or would she join the other skeletons with "completion dates" we'd seen in the dermestid tanks and on the walls in the apes' habitat?

"Let's go," Eric urged us. He pointed at the end of the hall, where a dark doorway loomed beneath a telltale red exit sign. "What are we waiting for?"

"Do you think this whole building has bugs in it?"

"Probably," said Savannah. "Every floor. Every room. I only hope they didn't escape."

"You guys," Eric said faintly, "this isn't funny anymore."

"Okay, Eric, we're leaving." I smirked at my best friend and we made for the exit sign.

The stairwell went up four landings and dead-ended at another door. I was at the head of the line, and when I saw what was written on the door, I stopped dead.

"Um, Eric, you might want to head back to the beetles."

He pushed past Savannah to see. "Why, what does it—" He paled, because beneath the red exit sign, this was what it said:

WARNING:
BEES
DO NOT ENTER WITHOUT PROTECTIVE GEAR

Eric threw his hands in the air in despair. "What is with this place? What kind of Shepherd keeps bees? Sheep, I understand."

"And chimps?" Savannah asked.

"And dermestids?" added Howard.

Eric turned to Howard. "No one should keep beetles, dude. Remind me to never go to your house again, now that I know what kind of monsters your dad thinks of as pets."

"That's not fair," said Howard. "They're Nate's, too."

"Have you ever heard of exterminators? People *pay* to get pests out of their houses."

"Pests like you?" Savannah teased. She looked at me. "Gillian, there's hope for your family."

I put my hands on my hips. "Okay, enough. Eric, do you want me to open this door or do you want to go back to the beetles?"

"I want to get to the beach," Eric said. "However I can. But I don't think I can handle bees."

"Okay," I said. "I'll check. Maybe the room will be empty like that Lady Bird one."

Carefully, I opened the door, bracing for buzzing, but the room beyond was silent. I ducked my head in and gasped, then opened the door wide.

"Eric," I said breathlessly, "I don't think you have to worry about the bees."

We entered the vast, open space. The room was several stories tall, and the ceiling was made of giant panes of dirty glass, which bathed us all in a sickly yellow light. It was late afternoon, and the sky must be a brilliant orange over the cove, but only the dregs made it into this forlorn, abandoned place.

Tall, narrow square columns stood in silent rows like forgotten monuments, some with missing panels that revealed gray-tinged honeycombs inside. There was a narrow metal walkway a foot or so off the floor that divided the room into a neat grid, with one of the giant white towers in the middle of each square. I realized they were beehives, though I'd never seen any this large. Below the walkways was a curdled, brownish mulch. I looked closer, then gasped.

The ground was a carpet of dead bees.

I guessed this entire room had reached its completion date.

I now realized why we hadn't been able to find a door to this building. The whole back wall looked like a giant automatic garage door. A red exit sign glowed dimly at the top.

By now, the Shepherd signs marking each experiment were almost familiar.

COLONY 2
REPRODUCTION RATE: IDEAL
POLLINATION EFFICIENCY: SATISFACTORY
SUBSTITUTION RATE: SATISFACTORY
RELEASE PENETRATION: COMPLETE
GUARANTEED COLLAPSE: SATISFACTORY
COMPLETION DATE:

COLONY 4:
REPRODUCTION RATE: UNSATISFACTORY
POLLINATION EFFICIENCY: IDEAL
SUBSTITUTION RATE: UNSATISFACTORY
RELEASE PENETRATION: INCOMPLETE
GUARANTEED COLLAPSE: IDEAL
COMPLETION DATE:

Weird. These colonies didn't have completion dates listed, but the bees inside were obviously dead. Every bee in this building was dead. I checked out a few more signs as we made our way across the metal walkways. Every step dislodged another shower of flaky bee carcasses onto the concrete below. Their wings sparkled with iridescence as they crumbled beneath our feet.

All the other experiments we'd found on the island were designed to help humans survive in space, but bees didn't fit the pattern. Why would anyone want to bring bees into space? They only made honey. You couldn't wear them, and you couldn't really live on honey, anyway. Not like—ick—moth jam.

"What's a 'guaranteed collapse'?" Eric asked as we passed another tower.

"I don't know." I examined the sign. Another overall satisfactory rating on a sign marking a hive full of dead bees. "Maybe it has something to do with colony collapse disorder?"

"What's that?" asked Savannah.

"It's that disease that bees have. You remember, the one Anton was talking about at dinner last night? Colony collapse disorder. The bees would just go off to gather pollen one day and never come back to their hive."

"Oh yeah," Eric said. "When all the bees started dying off, like, ten years ago. No one knows why. Some people blamed cell phones or new pesticides."

"Dad said it was Wi-Fi."

"No," said Eric. "Dad taught a class to his wacko friends saying it was Wi-Fi. There's a difference."

I was quickly learning that. Dad had taught me to be wary of people who wanted to track where people were going and what they were doing in the name of safety, but he'd been fine when Elana had done that exact thing in order to find us.

"Well, now we know why Anton was freaking out about it," I said. "He had a whole warehouse full of dead bees."

"Was there some kind of honey shortage I don't know about?" Savannah asked.

"Weren't you paying attention to Anton's lecture at dinner last night?"

"No," she replied, as if it were the most obvious thing in the world. "Because it was a lecture. At dinner."

"Honey is the smallest part of the problem," I said. "Most of the crops in this country depend on bees for pollination. Without bees, the plants don't make fruit. And the scary part is, since no one ever knew what caused the collapse, there's nothing we can do to prevent it from happening again."

Savannah frowned. "Poor bees. Maybe the Shepherds' research was on how to prevent it from happening. Maybe they were breeding bees who were immune."

"But then wouldn't they call it 'collapse resistance' instead of 'collapse guarantee' or whatever?"

She shrugged. "I have no idea why the Shepherds do what they do, Gillian. Isn't that what we're here to find out?"

Yes, but the more I learned about Eureka Cove, the more confused I got. I wished Dr. Underberg had given us a book to help unravel this puzzle, too. He wanted us to break their codes, and we had, but now what?

In the center of the room, the walkway widened into a small platform, on which sat a control panel as well as assorted screens and keyboards. "Oh, good, a command center. Maybe it'll tell us how to open those doors."

The panel was off, but when I pressed the power button, the machines hummed to life, echoing oddly in the dead space. All the buttons and dials were oversized and encased in heavy plastic, which I supposed made sense if they were designed to be operated by people wearing beekeeping suits.

A menu appeared on-screen:

HOME
OPERATIONS
SUBSTITUTION PENETRATION MAP
REPORTS

"Operations?" I guessed. I chose that option.

WATER
TEMPERATURE
CLEANING
RELEASE

"Release," Howard suggested from over my shoulder. But when I clicked, it wasn't the large cargo doors that opened, but instead a bank of tiny windows right under the translucent roof.

"Hmm." I went back to the home screen.

"I wonder what the penetration map is," I said.

"*Not* the way out." Eric tugged my sleeve. "Come on, Gills, quit stalling. I bet Dad is here already."

I clicked through anyway. Just one quick peek.

A multicolored map of the United States came up on-screen. Vast swaths of the map were shaded red and pink, with smaller segments in orange, yellow, green, and blue. To the right was a key marked *CCD Rate.* Red corresponded to 70 percent, pink to 60 percent, and so on. On the right, I could click through similar maps, labeled by colony and year.

"You're right," Savannah said, pointing at the key. "CCD, like colony collapse disorder. I guess they were trying to find a cure."

I bit my lip. The title of the map was "Substitution Penetration." But the only measurement seemed to show the rate of bees dying from colony collapse. I thought about the ratings on the signs: *Guaranteed Collapse.*

"I'm not so sure," I said.

"Gillian," Eric said in warning.

"One sec." I clicked over to the *Reports* section. A long list of documents filled the screen, each with a different date, and all from several years ago and marked "AE Update." The last one was marked "AE Conclusion."

"Seriously, Gills," said Eric. "If we're not out of here in ten seconds, I'm dragging you out by your hair. Ten . . ."

"Hold your horses!" If CCD was colony collapse disorder, then what was AE?

"Nine . . ."

I clicked on the conclusion.

By consensus of the board, Project Sweet Dreams has been terminated. All were in agreement that the principles of the project were sound. All main objectives were achieved. Strains exhibited excellent rates of penetration and substitution on release, and CCD rates peaked at 33 percent nationally, causing massive disruption of the agricultural chain and outcry for change at high levels.

Publicity for the campaign was also a success, with major coverage in both mainstream and alternative news, a documentary film, and even a major Hollywood disaster movie covering the phenomenon.

However, the effect on public consciousness has not lived up to expectations. Though there was an initial swell of interest, it has been determined that the consequences are either too subtle or too removed from day-to-day life to have any serious impact. (See also: global climate change.)

Future projects will focus on more immediate and noticeably disastrous effects. Board strongly feels that only panic will induce action on the part of humanity.—AE

Eric forgot about counting down and we all stared, openmouthed, at the screen.

"Wait," said Savannah. "Am I reading this right? They weren't trying to cure colony collapse disorder—"

"No." My throat seemed to choke on the words. "They *caused* it."

19

FREEZE!

FOR TWELVE YEARS, MY FATHER HAD TAUGHT ME ABOUT CONSPIRACY theories. He'd told me about the lies in my history books, about the way "They" twisted everything we knew to suit the facts they wanted known. He'd showed me how to spot the story behind the story. He'd made sure that I knew what kind of questions to ask to get beyond the standard excuses and find out the real truth. What about the cover story sounds fishy? Who stands to gain from making the public believe it? And, the biggie: Why are they doing all of this?

Usually, people kept secrets because telling the world the truth would send them into a panic. People liked nice, neat stories, where the bad guys got caught and the good guys were heroes and everyone turned out okay in the end.

But this—this was a conspiracy to *start* a panic.

I looked around this massive room, filled with tens of thousands of dead bees. Bees that had been bred to die—to go out and interbreed with normal bees, to substitute their faulty genetics, spread across the country, then conveniently die off, making everyone think there was a major problem with their pesticides or their cell phones or—if you were my father—their Wi-Fi signal.

And then what?

Board strongly feels that only panic will induce action on the part of humanity.—AE

AE: Anton Everett. I thought about dinner, about his passionate arguments to see the Earth as a world on the brink of destruction.

I'm trying to save humanity, he'd said. *The planet will go on.* He'd even sided with the Shepherds right in front of us, saying he agreed with them that the human race, as a whole, refused to see the danger staring us in the face. And he'd been right. All along, Anton was a Shepherd, sitting across the dinner table, telling us what he believed, and we hadn't seen it. Dani Alcestis was a Shepherd, and she'd gotten us invited to Guidant to give a talk in order to get us here and fulfill some Shepherd plot, and we came along like . . . well, like sheep.

Baa.

And as much as I hated to admit it, I saw Anton's point. No one liked change. As long as things were working, even if they weren't working great, most people would just muddle along the best they could. Like Mom and Dad, fighting over the way he'd get lost in his work, or whether or not the risks he took were worth it. It took some big, horrible crisis to change it all. The scandal, the flood, the weeks spent hiding out in the woods. That's when Mom finally had enough and decided to get out.

I wondered if that was what the Shepherds were trying to do by tampering with the Capella data. To push humanity to choose to get out, too. If we all thought an asteroid was coming toward Earth, we would definitely panic. And if we panicked enough, maybe we'd start to think more seriously about space. Maybe we'd start to behave the way the Shepherds wanted us to.

Elana had said Capella was her "pet project." I doubted she'd like her second-in-command's attempts to ruin it in order to help the Shepherds.

"You know what, Eric?" I turned to my brother. "You're right. We need to get out of here. Now."

"Freeze!" shouted a voice.

We whirled around to see four security guards standing on the walkway. Their uniforms were beige, with the Guidant logo on them. The guard in front held up her hand. "Hold on, it's the kids. We found them."

Behind me, Eric let out a sigh of relief. "Rescue."

I nudged him to keep quiet. For all we knew, these were just Shepherds in Guidant uniforms.

"Come with us," said the guard. "You have no idea how long we've been looking for you."

I didn't move. "Who sent you?"

She rolled her eyes. "Ms. Mero? Your father? It would have been way easier if you hadn't hung up on them before we figured out where you were going to meet. Now, come on. This island was dangerous *before* the trespassers came."

She must mean the trespassing Shepherds. I nodded, relieved that someone was finally on our side. Before we knew it, we were being hustled through an unseen exit near the cargo doors and down a few more flights of dimly lit stairs.

"I want to talk to my dad."

"We have to get you off the island," the guard said. There were two of them walking in front of us and two of them behind as we made our way down a sloping path of what looked like a basement tunnel. Pipes and wiring ran the length of the corridor, and the floor was nothing more than packed dirt. "Communication between here and the mainland is being monitored."

I shut my mouth.

At the end of the corridor, there was a large metal door,

fastened with a wheel, like a safe. One of the guards turned the wheel, unsealing the door, but it took two of them to pull it open. A gust of frigid air hit our faces, and with it, the dank smell of deep earth.

"Well," said Eric drily. "At least this looks familiar."

It did remind me of Omega City, and not just because we were clearly underground. Darkness stretched out around us, curved tiled walls and packed-earth floor receding into the distance. The only island of light was an inflatable enclosure about the size of our cottage sitting fifty feet away, glowing like a paper lantern in a moonless sky. Two large cargo trucks were parked in front of the door to the enclosure, and the guards led us toward them without delay.

"Is this a tunnel?" I asked one of them. "Does it go under the cove?"

She gave me a look and I shut up. Okay, I guess that was a stupid question. Of course it was a tunnel. And where else would it be going, if not under the cove? The island wasn't that big.

"I can't believe," she muttered, "that I've spent the entire day chasing down a bunch of children."

The guards stopped at the trucks.

"You kids stay here a second, while we check in. Do. Not. Move. Do you understand me?" She wagged her finger at us.

"Yes, ma'am," we mumbled as they departed.

Howard looked right, left, and then into the darkness above our heads. "We're turned around. We came farther inland, not out toward the beach. I bet we're right about under the chimp habitat."

Savannah cast me a worried glance. "I think we're in big trouble. Like, really big trouble."

"It'll be okay," I said, and toed the ground with my shoe. After all, I was still moving to Idaho. That was pretty much like being grounded, anyway.

"Can you get sent to jail for trespassing?" she asked. "I can't believe how far this went. All I wanted was to hang out with you as much as I could before you moved away."

"It'll be okay," I repeated, trying to convince myself as much as her. And it would. It should . . . once I explained to Dad what we'd learned about the Shepherds. Once we let Elana know about Anton and Dani.

As if my thoughts had summoned her, Dani Alcestis stepped out from behind the trucks. "Still here, huh? You guys are really bad at listening. Epically bad."

"Help!" I screamed. "Help, it's a Shepherd!"

The others joined in. "Help! Guards!"

Dani stood there serenely, arms crossed over her chest as we shouted. She was dry again, dressed in street clothes, her pretty lightened hair slicked back into a simple bun. She waited as our cries echoed through the chamber. "Are you done?"

The guards emerged from the inflatable enclosure, looking bewildered. I pointed at Dani. "She's a Shepherd! I saw her. We saw everything. You have to call my dad. The Shepherds are running all kinds of creepy experiments on the island. They killed the bees. They're trying to cause a panic! Please, you have to help us!"

The guard who'd been talking to us looked at Dani, seemingly baffled. "Miss Alcestis?"

Dani's expression was one of boredom. "Don't worry. I'll handle it. Finish your tasks."

We started shouting and pleading with the guards again, as all four climbed into the first cargo truck. We reached for the door handles as the truck's engines turned over, rumbling so loud I felt the ground shake beneath my feet. We only stepped back as they zoomed off, so as not to get run over. Their red brake lights retreated into the distance, and the trembling of the earth subsided. I wondered at that moment if that was what I'd felt when we'd been hiding in the chimp habitat.

Defeated, I turned back to Dani.

"'They killed the bees'? Is that seriously the best you could come up with? After all the time you've spent poking around here?"

"Well, you did," said Savannah. "And you killed those chimps, too."

Dani leaned in and glared at me. "I," she said slowly,

as if talking to an idiot, "told you"—she poked me in the chest—"to *run*."

"They didn't believe me," I said sadly, ignoring her. "They never believe us."

Dani groaned. "Are you kidding me?"

I glared up at her. "What's *your* problem?"

"Gillian," said Howard. "Don't you get it? They believed you. They're Shepherds, too."

A sense of utter horror washed over me. My knees felt weak, and I stumbled back from our captor. "What? No. They knew exactly what happened on the phone with Dad and . . ." I trailed off.

Oh, no. *Communication between here and the mainland is being monitored.* I replayed every word out of the guard's mouth on our trip here.

You have no idea how long we've been looking for you. Ever since they'd found our kayaks, no doubt.

It would have been easier if you hadn't hung up on them before we figured out where you were going to meet. No wonder she'd said "them."

This island was dangerous before the trespassers came. Those trespassers . . . were *us*.

She hadn't lied. She'd just told us exactly what we'd wanted to hear.

Dani rapped me on the head with her knuckles. "Figured it out yet, Little Miss Know-It-All?"

"Hey!" Eric cried. "Back off, lady!"

To my surprise, she did just that, stepping back and giving us a once-over as she shook her head with pity. "What in the world did you think you were doing in the entomology center, playing with all the controls? This isn't Omega City, you know. We can tell when you're accessing our files. You should have just stayed away from this place. Played on the smart courts or gone boating, *like I suggested.*"

I straightened. "We did go boating. We kayaked right over here."

"This isn't a game, don't you get that? And it's certainly not for kids, whatever he might have led you to think."

He? Did she mean Dad? "Well, if we can figure out what you're up to, then Dad and Elana can, too. It must have killed you that Elana wanted someone like my father here at Eureka Cove. You Shepherds can't hide much longer."

"Oh, Elana wanted your father here, all right, but not for the reason you think."

"What?" I asked.

Dani sighed. "I don't even know what I'm supposed to do now. You've put me in a very difficult position. I don't like the choices I'm going to have to make."

Her words sent a chill down my spine. Was she going to hurt us? All my bluster fled. "Please," I said. "Please, we just want to get back to my dad. We just want to go home."

"'Home?'" she scoffed. "'*Please*?' Do you think politeness gets you far with the Shepherds? Or being children? I read your father's book. Fiona Smythe warned you. Underberg warned you. Yet here we are." She shook her head. "This makes it all so much more complicated. What am I supposed to do, claim I've lost you?" Dani's eyes flicked from one of us to the next, observing carefully, as if weighing our worth. Something beeped on her wrist.

"I'll be right there," she said into the band, then turned back to us. "Okay. Come with me. Now, or you'll be sorry."

Exchanging worried glances, we let Dani herd us to the door of the inflatable enclosure. It was shaped like a giant beached jellyfish, an amorphous white bubble banded by arcs of steel. She held open the door as if she were still our Guidant hostess and gestured for us to come inside.

"Do you like it?" she asked as we blinked in the sudden brightness. "It's Guidant's own design. A pop-up biostation. Able to be assembled and disassembled in less than three hours. Totally self-contained and solar-powered, not that we can charge it up down here."

I squinted. It was like standing inside a seashell. White walls, as thin and as taut as sails, separated the station into oblong chambers. Dani led us down a narrow central corridor. The whole place hummed.

"Battery backups in case of power loss—or underground use—automatic air filters and water collection, not to mention sealing capabilities in case of a plague or biochemical attack."

Was she kidnapping us or trying to sell us one? I took a quick glance in one of the rooms we passed and saw what looked like an operating table surrounded by a bank of brushed steel lockers.

"The floors, you will note, are made of the same customizable material as the smart courts." She glanced meaningfully at our utility suits.

Our utility suits, which were invisible to their sensors. Wait a second. . . . I grabbed Savannah's arm and squeezed. Was Dani saying what I thought she was saying?

Was she trying to help us escape?

All this time, I was sure that Dani was a Shepherd ringleader. And maybe she was, but she had also told us to run before. Maybe she was taking pity on us because we were kids or something. Maybe we still had a chance to escape. I'd messed up bad with those guards in the bee chamber. I didn't want to risk getting it wrong again.

She led us into the last room at the end of the hall. "Of course, the problem with infrared sensors is that they rely on the presence of heat, which in an operation like ours, is not as common as it might otherwise be." As soon as we were all over the threshold, she unfolded an accordion door and hooked it across the opening, closing all five of us inside.

The room was small and sparse, and there was barely room for anything more than a computer terminal and an exam table. This one was topped with what looked like a large, inflatable blue mattress, covered with a sheet and riddled with wires.

Dani turned to face us, folding her hands in front of her. "Any questions, kids?"

"Are you serious?" Eric blurted.

"Eric," I said in warning.

"No, Gills. We've been all over this island and we still don't have any idea what's going on. And she's standing here making vague threats—"

"Mr. Seagret," Dani broke in. "Did it ever occur to you that's because anything other than vague means we'd all get ourselves killed? Thanks to your sister's brilliant tattling up at the radio station, our entire operation is in danger." She sighed. "Now, if you will excuse me, I've got some very important matters I need to see to." She nodded at the table in our midst. "And so do you."

With that, she slipped back through the opening of the chamber and left us alone, staring at one another in shock across the inflatable mattress.

"I don't understand," said Howard. "Right?"

"Yes," Savannah assured him. "No one here does."

"Is she . . ." Eric lifted his shoulders. "Is she trying to save our lives?"

"She's definitely telling us to escape," I said, looking down at my utility suit. "And I think she's telling us how, but . . ." I put my hand on top of the mattress.

But instead of a taut, cushy surface, the sheet crumpled inward, as if the center of the mattress was hollow. And whatever was beneath the sheet felt . . .

Alive.

I shuddered. "There's something in there." And it was cold as ice.

"Take off the sheet," said Savannah.

"No way." I stepped back, stumbling over my feet until I hit the fabric wall. I did not want to know what was under there. My hand tingled where I'd touched it, frigid as a corpse.

"Eric," Savannah said. "Take off the sheet."

"You first," Eric suggested.

Howard shook his head. "I'll do it." He pulled back the fabric.

Underneath was a chimpanzee.

20

UNDERCOVER

THE INSIDE OF THE MATTRESS WAS INDEED HOLLOW, AND FITTED TO HOLD the chimp's body securely in place. I'd never seen a chimp laid out like that. It really did look like a naked, furry human. I mean—*she* did. This one was apparently a female. Thick gel pads covered the chimp's legs and chest, and her head was fitted with a gel cap. An air mask covered her mouth, and wires and monitors were stuck to her head and chest.

"This is the chimp we saw captured." Savannah reached out her hand and touched the animal. "She's freezing."

"How can you tell?" Eric asked.

"Because she feels cold," Sav snapped.

"No, I mean, how do you know she's the one . . ." Eric held up his hands and averted his eyes from the chimp's nether regions. "Never mind. I don't want to know."

Howard turned on the computer screen as Savannah continued to examine the chimp. The gel pads spread across her body were, in fact, ice packs, like the kind you use for sore muscles, and the inflatable cushion she was lying in was also cold to the touch.

The display on-screen showed the chimp's heart rate, breathing, and metabolic activity. There were two lines being traced. One in green, marked *normal,* and another one, in blue, marked *experimental.*

"I think," Howard began slowly, "I think they have her in hibernation."

"Cool!" said Eric. "They froze her! I thought they needed a tank or something for that."

"Not cryogenic freezing, you dolt," I said. "*Hibernation.* You know, like a bear in the winter."

"Chimps don't hibernate," Savannah said.

"Neither do humans," Howard pointed out. "But a lot of people are trying to find a way to put our bodies in a hibernation state for space travel. Basically, they induce medical hypothermia so we don't need to breathe as much, or eat, or even move. It's called torpor."

"Hypothermia?" Savannah made a face. "Doesn't that kill you?"

"If it happens on a mountain or something, then yes, sometimes. But if hypothermic torpor is induced in a hospital, under strict medical conditions, or on a spaceship . . ." Howard shrugged. "It's only experimental at this point. We don't know if we can do it for a long time without causing permanent brain damage, for instance. They still need to test it."

Savannah straightened. "Wait. How would they test something like that? Would they put you in torpor or whatever, then thaw you out and, like, give you a test to see if your brain's okay?"

Howard shrugged. "I guess."

Savannah's eyes got huge, and she hurriedly unzipped the pocket of her suit and pulled out a sheaf of papers. "Look! The intelligence tests I told you about in the chimp habitat."

She showed me the papers. There was a column for test score, and a column called "duration." One day, ten days, thirty days, fifty . . .

"What if they froze the chimps . . ."

"Put them in hypothermic torpor," Howard corrected.

"What difference does it make?" she asked him.

"Fine," he said. "What if they froze the *monkeys* . . ."

She glared at him, then went on. "Put them up in space for a while, then they thawed them out and gave them the tests again to see if they had brain damage." She pulled out one sheet. "Look, this is her." She pointed to an ID number at the top of the sheet, which matched the one onscreen. "She's passed all the tests so far. So this one would be for . . ." Her face fell. "Oh. Bone density loss. That was always the last test."

Right. The tanks full of flesh-eating beetles and the picked-clean skeletons. "You mean they're going to kill her after this and test her bone density?"

Savannah pursed her lips. "Oh, no, they're not." She headed to the terminal controlling the monitors. "Howard, help me find how to turn it off."

He held up his hands. "I have no idea."

"Savannah," I said, "we don't have time for this. We have to get out of here."

"Yeah," she said. "We *all* have to get out of here."

I looked down at the sleeping chimpanzee. "What are we going to do with a chimpanzee?"

"Take her back to the others."

"They aren't safe in that habitat," I said.

"Well, it's better than here!" She turned to my brother. "Can you help me figure this out?"

Eric looked at her, then nodded. "Okay." He gave me a shrug. "She's right, we can't just leave her here."

I shook my head in disbelief. There was no guarantee we could even get out, let alone help a half-frozen chimp. And we weren't going back to the chimp habitat, anyway.

We needed to get to the mainland and find my father. "The only way we can sneak out of here is with our utility suits. And we don't have extras."

"You heard Dani. They're infrared sensors," Savannah said. "If we get the chimp out while she's still pretty cold, she won't show up on their monitors."

"You plan to carry her?" I asked. "She must weigh a hundred pounds."

Savannah's shoulders slumped. "Maybe we can sling her between us, or find a cart. . . ."

"I'll carry her." Eric looked up from his keyboard at our incredulous faces. "What? I've been working out all summer." Then—wait, was that a blush on his face?—he turned back to the screen. "Look: initiate warming. That must be it, right?"

"Yes!" Savannah tapped the keys.

A message popped up on-screen.

This action will terminate hypothermic period. Do not disengage subject from cooling station until directed to do so. Continue? YES/NO

"Uh-oh," said Savannah. "I thought we could just unplug her and run."

Howard had pulled out a bunch of bungee cords and his carabiners. "Look, Eric. I bet I can rig up these cords and this sheet to sort of strap her to you."

"That's the least of our problems," I said. "Remember what Dani told us. They found us in the beehive room because we were playing with the computers. They are monitoring everything. If we unplug her, they'll know."

Savannah considered this for a moment. "I don't care." She clicked the button.

The mattress began to hum and deflate. A new message popped up on the screen.

Please fold back cooling pads during deflation to prevent tangling. Disconnecting subject from station before warming period is complete will result in loss of data.

"Oh," I said. "Is that all? Well, who cares about the Shepherds getting their stupid data? Let's steal this chimp."

Savannah pumped her fist in the air. "Yes!"

Quickly, the boys rigged some kind of sling to help Eric carry the chimp, while Savannah and I folded back the ice packs and removed her air mask. Her fur was soft, not as wiry as it looked, though her skin was still creepily cold to the touch. Someone had shaved patches of fur off her skin so the monitors could attach more smoothly, leaving weird bald spots all over her head and tummy. I winced as I peeled the monitors off her body, half expecting an alarm to sound as soon as the computer lost its input source.

Finally, she was free from the machine, but still ice-cold and unconscious. I supposed the unconscious part was good, though. Less poop flinging.

"Okay," I said to Eric. "It's now or never."

It took all three of us to hoist the chimp onto Eric's back. We tied her arms around Eric's neck and positioned her legs around his waist, piggyback style. Then Howard wrapped the sheet around her and bungee-corded the whole thing together. By the time he was done, Eric looked like an enormous blue humpback.

"Good?" Howard asked.

Eric puffed and held up his thumb, but I noticed his face looked pained.

"Can you run like that?"

"Um . . ." He grunted and adjusted the load. "Let's start with walking. And hope there's an elevator."

An elevator? "Yeah, because that worked so well for us in Omega City."

Eric looked traumatized.

"Don't listen to her, Eric," Savannah said. "This place is in much better shape than Omega City was. They didn't carry this chimp down a flight of stairs."

"Great. So, first things first. Find the elevator."

"Hoods up," said Howard. "We have to hide from the infrared." He unrolled his own hood, and Savannah and I did the same, then helped Eric get his on.

Howard stuck his head out of the chamber, then motioned for us to follow. We hurried back to the front door. I checked inside each chamber as we passed. Every one featured one of those cooling mattresses. How many chimps were they planning on freezing?

"Look!" Savannah pointed in triumph. Inside the front door was posted a diagram of the underground space. We were in the building marked *Biostation*. A long tunnel stretched in front of us with an arrow marked *To Eureka Cove*.

That was the direction the guards had taken their truck. It must be the tunnel that went under the water and back to the Guidant campus. There were also three smaller tunnels, one marked *Botany*, one marked *Entomology*, and one marked *Bacteria*.

I pointed at Entomology. "We came through this tunnel. Entomology means the study of bugs."

Eric shifted uncomfortably. "We aren't going back that way."

Behind the biostation was a small square that said *To CRC*.

"Chimp Research Center," Savannah said. "Let's go."

We circled the outside of the station, our figures casting long, ghostly shadows on the floor of the cavern as we hugged close to its glowing, jellyfish sides.

"You okay?" I said to Eric, who was panting heavily.

"Fine," he said, in a tone that meant definitely not.

Around back, the cavern continued for another ten yards or so, then ended in a reinforced wall. In the center sat the large silver cage doors of a cargo elevator. We climbed inside, pulled the doors shut, and pressed the button marked *Dome*.

Howard nudged me, then gestured up to the corner of the ceiling, where there was a camera.

I raised my finger to my visor, as if putting it on my lips. He nodded and we nudged the others. If it wasn't an infrared camera, we were in real trouble.

A minute later, the elevator screeched to a stop. We hauled open the doors to find ourselves in a nondescript room.

"Where's the dome?" Eric asked desperately. "I don't know how much farther I can go."

"Here! Here!" Savannah danced down to another door. She opened it to reveal the wrecked-out hall of the observation lounge where we'd first met the apes. "Quick."

We hustled into the hall, where the skeletons of the space chimps stared down at us with menace. The sun had set by now, and the dome was growing dark. I kept a wary eye on the habitat inside the dome, but there was no sign of the other apes, or their poop. Nevertheless, I planned to keep my visor up.

"Help me," Eric said, standing at the divider separating

the lounge from the domed habitat. I climbed over the barrier, then gave him a hand as he stumbled across. Savannah followed.

There was a rustling in the leaves behind me. I braced myself for getting pummeled with poop, but nothing happened.

With Savannah's help, we loosened the chimp from her bindings and she fell off Eric's back in a tangled heap.

"Oof," Savannah said.

Eric dropped to his knees. "I think I broke my back."

"Just rest for a second." She got him situated, then turned around to straighten the chimp's limbs. Howard was still in the observation lounge, keeping watch for any Shepherds.

Savannah bent over the ape, adjusting her limbs and petting her thick black hair like she was tucking her in to bed. The chimp looked relaxed, but I was leaping out of my skin. I clasped my hands together. "We have to get out of here."

"Gillian," Eric begged. "I seriously can't move. Unless you plan to carry me, I need a break."

I sighed. There was no way I could carry him for more than a few feet. "Okay." I sat down next to him, inside the dome, our backs to the barrier.

Savannah joined us. "I have no idea how long it will take for her to wake up. I did manage to find a pulse, though. And she's breathing. Should we wait?"

"We have to wait at least a little," I said. "Eric needs some time to recover." I didn't want to say what I was thinking. Chances were good that by rescuing this chimp, we were giving up our only opportunity to escape. But it was too late to do anything about it now.

Several minutes passed in silence, and I thought about the Shepherds. If Howard was right, they were doing hibernation experiments on the chimps to see how long-term hypothermic torpor would affect human health and mental ability. Just like the original space program had used chimps like Ham and Enos to see if humans could survive the stress of space travel, the Shepherds were testing their descendants to see if they could survive long-term hibernation.

And if those coded messages were right, then the Shepherds were tampering with the data from the Capella project to trick people into thinking there was an asteroid headed to Earth. Anton's work with the bees had been a bust, so they needed something to cause widespread panic.

And then what? Convince humanity to put all their resources into international space travel? That might work for a little while, but based on what I'd seen on the island, even with all the Shepherds' work on pygmy sheep and jammy silkworms and frozen monkeys, we weren't ready to settle down on Mars quite yet. So unless they kept occasionally threatening us with nonexistent asteroids, we'd eventually calm down again. Long before the human race decided to pack up and move out.

So what was this really all about? And why was Dani so frantic about it?

Far above the top of the tree, the sky had turned a deep indigo, and stars were just starting to twinkle to life. Howard joined us, tilting his face upward toward the heavens.

"It looks like Omega City," he said.

I examined the sky and the broken domed roof. "You're right. It does a little."

"I miss it," he said. "I sometimes dream I'm back there."

"Me, too," said Eric. "I call them nightmares."

I elbowed him.

"Sorry, but it's true."

Howard said nothing for a bit. And then, "Do you think he's up there?" He meant Dr. Underberg.

I stared at the vast, endless expanse of midnight blue. "I don't know anymore."

And I didn't know what Dr. Underberg had been trying to say when he'd sent Howard that book. If he'd wanted to let us know about the Shepherds at Eureka Cove, surely there was a better way than trying to get us to discover and decode their messages ourselves.

That was just like Dr. Underberg, though. First he'd left behind that riddle of a treasure map leading to Omega

City, and now his stupid code book. Another test, as if the only thing he really cared about was seeing if we were smart enough to play his game.

But Dani had been right about one thing: this wasn't a game. And it was way too big for kids like us to play.

I sat up suddenly, remembering what my father had said—why would the Shepherds' codes be something easy enough for kids like us to break? Kids like us, who'd just gotten our first code-breaking book the night before?

They wouldn't. It was as simple as that. Just like Dr. Underberg's treasure map to Omega City, a puzzle that Fiona couldn't figure out, but that we managed to solve in a single afternoon, because we had all the pieces. He hadn't made it to be impossible. He'd made it for his friends.

Friends like us.

I thought about the messages we'd decoded.

Shepherds ready to move on target at Eureka Cove.

I agreed with Dad this morning. A Shepherd wouldn't say something like that to another Shepherd. They'd just say, We *are ready to move.*

If Dani hadn't been sending the messages to other Shepherds, who had she been talking to? Who was the friend her codes were for?

"Howard?" I asked. "Where are the codes we took from the station?"

"Here, let me get them. . . ." Howard dug the papers

out of his pockets and handed them to me.

Seagrets accepted invitation to speak at Guidant. Please advise.

Need confirmation of Capella tampering. Expect counterattack.

Infinity Base not secure. Prepare for evacuation—

Savannah clamped a hand down on my arm. "Watch."

I looked to see the fur shifting on our chimpanzee friend. I wasn't sure if she was waking, or if a breeze had ruffled her hair.

After a few more minutes, something else stirred. A tiny figure emerged from the shadow of the tree—the baby chimp. It came out a few steps, chittering plaintively.

"Aw," said Savannah. "It wants its mommy."

None of us moved a muscle. The mama chimp lay on her sheet, several yards away, and the baby sat halfway between the tree and its mother, clearly too scared to come forward.

At long last, the chimp rolled over. I saw her face the baby and weakly extend an arm. The baby retreated with a little shriek. The mother hooted softly at it, arm still outstretched. For a few seconds, the baby hopped back and forth, undecided. The mother didn't move, just lay there, repeating her murmured invitation.

We sat there, transfixed. I had no idea how long this went on, the baby, trembling with fear and distrust, as the mama chimp held her arms open, as if she would wait for all eternity.

"Go on," whispered Savannah.

I swallowed thickly, unable to speak.

Finally, with aching slowness, the chimp crawled forward into the curl of its mother's arms. She held it close.

The wind wafted around us, bringing the sounds of summer insects, as we watched the chimps together. I had no idea what the future held for them. We hadn't saved her from the Shepherds. They could just as easily repeat their experiment tomorrow and drag her away again. But for now she was with her child, and that was enough.

Beneath the protection of my visor, my cheeks were wet.

I had just started thinking it was time to get a move on when the sound of footfalls startled us all. The chimp lumbered to her feet and limped off as quickly as her sluggish muscles could carry her, her baby clinging to her fur. We scrambled to our feet and turned to face the intruder.

"Good," said Dani. This time she was wearing what looked for all the world like an Omega City utility suit. "I'd hoped I'd find you here." She nodded toward the chimp. "I see you took the bait. I knew you would. Softies."

"What are you doing to these chimps?" Savannah asked, her tone accusing.

Dani lifted her shoulders in a shrug. "The same things

hundreds of companies do to thousands of chimps all over the world. The same thing Howard's precious NASA did to those skeletons up on the wall. The same thing humans do to every other life form on the planet. Use them for our own purposes. In this case, we were doing a study of the detrimental effects of long-term hypothermic torpor on brain function and body mass." She shrugged. "Better them than us."

"I knew it," I said, indignant.

She gave me a sour glance. "Aren't you clever." Dani stepped over the barrier and into the dome. "Well, I'm here with some bad news."

"What, this time you really have to take us in?"

"No. But I'm afraid I'll soon have to tender my resignation at Guidant. Unfortunately, thanks to our little adventure back there at the biostation, they're onto me."

"Oh, no," I snapped. "Poor you, going to lose your job if they find out you're a Shepherd. How does it feel?"

"If they find out I'm a Shepherd?" she echoed. This time, her laugh was real. "Gillian, we're *all* Shepherds here."

"Wait, really?" Eric asked. I expected a jolt of surprise, but all I felt was sick to my stomach as the last shreds of hope vanished. Of course they were. Of course. Dad was never going to be okay. None of us were.

"That's the whole point of this company. The Arkadia

Group had to hide when Underberg went rogue, but it never disappeared. Everyone in a leadership position in Guidant is a Shepherd. Come on. Guidant? Herding? Isn't it obvious?"

"Ohhh," Savannah said, thoughtful. "Yeah, now that you put it like that, it is."

"So Elana Mero is a Shepherd," I said coldly.

She rolled her eyes. "Elana is at the top of the heap. That's why I freaked out when you told her about my messages."

"But you're a Shepherd, too!" I said, confused.

"Yes," she said with a shrug. "Pretty much since birth. Kind of came with the territory. But that doesn't mean I'm not on your side."

"What side?" Eric asked.

"Aloysius Underberg's, of course!" Dani replied. "He's my father."

21 UNDERBERGS

IT TURNED OUT DANI HAD WANTED TO MEET US IN THE DOME FOR A VERY specific reason.

"This is the only place on the island where we can talk freely," she said. "Everything is broken here, and they can't monitor us. With the help of our utility suits, their drones won't be able to spot us on their infrared cameras, either."

"Why is this place in ruins if the Shepherds are still doing experiments here?" I asked.

Dani looked pained. "Because it was easy to construct, but not to keep up. Guidant money built this place; then Elana claimed it wasn't energy efficient to do things out here. It was an easy excuse to shut it down so the Shepherds could take over the facilities with no one noticing. We had our own private tunnels to get in and out, so no outsiders—no one in Eureka Cove who wasn't involved in our operations—would even notice us coming and going. There are enough Guidant employees who are also Shepherds to keep the whole thing a secret." She glanced around the ruins of the dome. "We let ivy grow over all the buildings, so on the off chance that someone ended up here or photographed it from above, it would look like what we claimed it was—abandoned."

"But this chimp habitat is more than abandoned," Savannah said. "It's in ruins."

"That is unfortunate," Dani agreed. She rooted around in her pockets and pulled out a few packets of astronaut ice cream. "Hungry?"

"Starved!" Eric and Howard snatched the packets out of her hands.

"It's an old family recipe," she said with a grin.

I narrowed my eyes. There was no way this pretty young woman was Dr. Underberg's daughter. He was an old man. And besides, she looked nothing like him.

She caught me glaring. "We'll get to my story in a minute, Gillian. I promise you, it's true. Anyway, Savannah, to answer your question, the dome was supposed to be intact. I used to work in this center. But a few years ago we had an accident in one of our facilities. It sent a shock wave through the island and broke the dome. Unfortunately, we couldn't get it repaired. We'd need cranes and all kinds of construction materials, and remember, we were operating in secret, so . . . it ended up going a little wild."

"But that's not safe for the chimps," Savannah insisted. "What about the winters?"

"There's enough shelter in winter for them to be okay," she said. "They could always come inside the main building, too."

"Why didn't they escape?" asked Eric.

"Escape where? We're on an island." Dani opened up a packet of ice cream. "Plus, we made sure they were conditioned not to leave the center."

"Conditioned?" Savannah looked indignant. "How?"

Dani didn't even look contrite. "We shocked them if they tried to leave. Ice cream?"

Savannah turned her nose up at the offer. I didn't blame her. Those poor monkeys hadn't done anything, and they were left to fend practically for themselves in a ruin. And Dani thought she could make it all better with some powdered treats?

"Tell us what you're doing here," I said. "I don't believe you're really an Underberg."

"I'm not," she replied primly. "I'm an Alcestis. My mother was a computer scientist. Once upon a time, she and my father were both Shepherds, but then he lost faith in the group's mission. The Shepherds don't take too kindly to people who act against them, as your family discovered. They drummed my father—Dr. Underberg—out of their organization, and gave my mom the choice about whether to join him and go on the run or stay with them." She looked down. "I was just a baby. The Shepherds offered her security, so she took it. I don't blame her."

"She abandoned your father?" Sounded familiar. What was with moms?

"She took care of her child," Dani corrected. "What was the alternative, hide out in Omega City, get raised underground? No thank you."

"Makes sense to me," said Eric.

But I just sniffed. Dr. Underberg had managed it. "So they turned you into a Shepherd."

"If that's the way you want to see it. The Shepherds aren't totally bad, you know. Your precious Dr. Underberg used to be one."

"Isn't he *your* precious Dr. Underberg?" Howard asked. "He is your father."

"I don't remember him," Dani answered. "You all have seen him more than I have. I've never even spoken to the man face-to-face. I grew up with my mom and became a scientist like she was. My mother died when I was a teenager, but the Shepherds are like family, if you're loyal. I took a job as Elana's assistant, but mostly I did research for the Shepherds and reported back to Elana."

"What kind of research?"

"Do you know what it is the Shepherds do?"

"Yes," I snapped. "They destroy people's lives to further their own goals." That's what they'd done to my father. That was what they'd done to *hers*.

"Sometimes," she admitted, after a moment. "People need guidance. But Shepherds aren't in it for themselves. We're doing our job for the good of the flock. We're here to save the human race."

"What about those dead bees? How was that going to save anything?"

"Right, well, that was Anton's idea. You see, the Shepherds want to expand the flock, to herd humanity to greener pastures. We want to make sure that the human race survives anything that time and misfortune might throw at it. That's why my father was such a perfect addition to our ranks. He also wanted to help the human race survive. That's why he built Omega City, as a fail-safe."

"But the Shepherds don't want us to stay on Earth."

"Exactly. They didn't agree with Dr. Underberg that there was any hope for us here. During the Cold War, they were sure we'd destroy the planet, and that our only salvation would be in outer space."

"Do they still think that?" Howard asked.

"You heard Elana and Anton the other night. It's not like they hide it."

"We didn't know they were Shepherds," said Eric.

"Oh," Dani said. "Interesting. So according to you, the problem isn't what Elana and Anton think, it's that you've already decided Shepherds are the bad guys."

Yes, I thought. But what I said was, "The problem is that you're lying about asteroids, and killing bees and chimpanzees, and kidnapping people!"

Dani nodded. "I agree with you. *That* is the problem. And it's because of people like Anton. He was raised in the organization, just like me, and he's getting impatient. He doesn't think we're heading into space fast enough. I think he always believed, when we were growing up, that we'd have colonies on Mars by now."

"Yes!" Howard exclaimed.

Dani gave him a weak smile. "You actually remind me a lot of him."

"Except Howard would never do anything to hurt the planet, just to send us into space," I said defiantly. "Right, Howard?"

"I don't know if you really want the answer to that," said Eric, and he was probably right.

"It's where I stopped agreeing with the Shepherds, too," Dani pointed out. "I want to get to space, don't get me wrong, but I have no interest in poisoning the well. Earth has enough problems as it is. We shouldn't do anything to make it worse."

"So," Savannah said, "you're a double agent?"

"I didn't know where to go," she said. "There aren't a lot of people you can turn to if you go against the Shepherds. Then Sam Seagret published his book. Your family was a target of the Shepherds, but instead of disappearing, you fought back. You even found my father."

"So we're not idiots after all?" I asked sarcastically.

"Sorry," she said. "I was angry. You haven't been very discreet since you got here. You practically told Elana about the numbers station."

The numbers station, where I now realized Dani had never been sending messages to the other Shepherds.

Seagrets accepted invitation to speak at Guidant. Please advise.

"Wait a second." I held up the sheets we'd stolen from the station. "These messages . . . They were for Dr. Underberg?"

And that was why he'd given Howard the code book. He wanted us to listen in.

Dani nodded. "It's how my parents communicated all those years. It was a brilliant system—public but untraceable. Mom taught me how to decode them using their old letters. They used to love sending each other coded messages. He stopped writing to us after Mom died, and I figured he'd passed away, too, until I read your father's book. So I sent him a message, using the old code, and he responded. We've been talking ever since. I've been keeping him up to date on the Shepherds' plans, and he's been doing whatever he can to stop them."

"I knew he was okay," I said.

"Of course," she replied. "Aloysius Underberg is the world's leading expert on survival. You don't think something like a rocket-ship launch could kill him, do you?"

"So are you the one who sent me the code book?" Howard asked.

Dani made a face, crumpled up the ice cream wrapper, and stuck it back in her pocket. She wouldn't even litter in this wreck of a habitat. "No. Apparently Underberg doesn't trust me enough to keep me entirely in the loop. I have no idea how you got that book, though I have a few suspicions."

"So there are other people on this"—Savannah gestured vaguely to our little group—"team?"

"We're not a team," I insisted.

Dani chuckled. "I'm inclined to agree with you, but my father doesn't see it that way. And Elana is taking advantage of that."

"What do you mean?"

"She's recruiting your father."

"Dad would never be a Shepherd," I stated.

Dani's expression was filled with pity. "That's cute."

I bristled. "He wouldn't! The Shepherds tried to destroy our lives."

"Haven't you wondered why the Shepherds never tried again?"

Well, actually, yes I had. We all had. Even Mom.

"If you can't beat 'em, join 'em, Gillian," said Dani. "We ruined your father before he found Omega City, but he was very persistent. *You* were very persistent. So we had to step it up a notch. If threatening your dad didn't put him off his research, then the next best thing to do would be to distract him."

"Offer him a job," said Eric softly.

Wow. Mom had been even more right than I'd thought.

"And honestly, I thought that was the end of it," she said. "But Elana's plan was more devious than I expected. I thought she just wanted to get you guys to side with her. But Underberg is threatening to sabotage her Capella project."

"Is that what Dr. Underberg is doing up in space?" Howard asked. "He's getting proof that the satellite data is being tampered with?"

Dani looked at him curiously, and her next words hit me like a punch in the gut. "What satellite?"

I gasped. "Wait a second. Are you saying that Guidant never put a satellite in space?" That was insane. Everyone had seen their images! Just last week Howard and I had listened to stories about how they'd discovered asteroids only a few hundred thousand miles from Earth!

"They put *something* in space," said Dani. "And Dr. Underberg is threatening to expose the truth."

I wasn't sure I wanted to know. A spy satellite, to monitor everyone on Earth? A giant missile launcher, to rain down bombs from above?

Dani went on. "Elana is desperate to stop him, and for that, she needs leverage."

"What do you mean?"

Dani sighed. "For whatever reason, my father is very protective of you. That means you aren't recruits, Gillian. You're hostages. And unless Underberg does what the Shepherds want, you're in big trouble."

SAVANNAH DIDN'T WANT to leave the chimpanzees "unprotected," but Dani convinced her that she was in no position to play guard. After all, she was pretty much a captive herself. Our only goal now was to figure out how to get away from the Shepherds and find my dad before Elana decided to make an example of him to Dr. Underberg.

Dani was skeptical of this. "Last I heard, they were

transporting him to the biostation."

"Then we have to go!" I exclaimed. "We have to get my dad."

Dani shook her head. "To be honest, I'm not sure we can. I'm not even sure we can get you guys out safely. I'm sure your dad wouldn't like it if you risked yourselves to—"

"No!" I shouted. "We have to." I looked at Eric. "Right?"

He nodded firmly. "Yes. We have to." Savannah and Howard nodded, too.

Dani scowled. "Fine. But it's your funeral."

Together, we headed back into the elevator and down to the biostation.

"Be careful," Dani said to us as we exited. "If you get caught again, I can't help you or they'll nail me for sure."

We crept around the edge of the biostation. Parked out front were several electric cars and a large truck like a moving van, with personnel loading equipment and long gray containers into the cargo area. I caught sight of Elana Mero in a smart black pantsuit, standing in the midst of the activity.

Dani let out a mumbled curse, then pushed us all back behind the edge of the enclosure. "We're later than I thought. You should have just let him go."

Let Dad go? Easy for her to say. She'd never even met her father.

Quickly, Dani discarded her utility suit, leaving her dressed in the pants and shirt she'd worn earlier. She strode out from our hiding spot, her posture casual and commanding.

"Elana!" she called brightly.

"There you are!" Her boss came over. "Where have you been?"

"Dealing with the kids. They're neutralized."

"Do you have them in pods?"

"Oh!" Dani sounded surprised. "No . . . I didn't realize you were sending them to Infinity Base."

Elana groaned in frustration. "That crazy old man. He's not giving us any choice. I will not let him ruin what I've worked for all these years, even if I have to destroy Infinity Base to do it."

"Why can't you leave them?" Dani pressed.

"You know the answer to that," Elana said, and patted Dani on the arm. "Underberg has always had a soft spot for children. It's the only way we've ever been able to control him."

Dani said nothing. I reached out blindly for Eric's hand and squeezed, hard.

After a moment, Dani seemed to find her voice. "We could just make it look—"

Elana threw up her hands in frustration and stormed

off. "I don't want to hear it. I've already had a horrible day. I swear, Dani, if you thought the kids were bad, you should have seen the mother. . . ."

They entered the enclosure, still talking.

"Gills? Gills. Gills, Gills, Gills . . ." Eric tugged my sleeve. "What is she saying? What are pods? What's Infinity Base?"

"I don't know." I felt cold, and it had nothing to do with the cooling setting on my utility suit.

If you thought the kids were bad, you should have seen the mother. . . .

We kept in the shadows as Shepherds swarmed the area in front of the station, packing supplies in long narrow boxes into the cargo truck. When they were done, they piled into the cars and and drove off in the direction of the Eureka Cove campus. When only the truck remained, Elana and Dani emerged from the station. I risked taking a half step out of the shadows so that I could catch their conversation.

"We'll have to come back with the last load of pods," Elana was saying. "Do you think the others will be ready in time?"

"Oh, without a doubt," Dani said. She looked over her boss's shoulder and met my eyes, then glanced pointedly at the door to the station. Her intent was clear.

Inside.

Elana climbed into the cab of the truck, while Dani began talking animatedly to the driver. As soon as I was sure she had the driver distracted, I motioned to the others, and we hurried around the side of the biostation to the front door. We slipped inside, then stopped dead.

The place looked completely different than it had only an hour or two before. Instead of a bunch of tiny chambers, the interior was entirely open, a giant, glowing white bubble. At the far opposite end stood five of the cooling station tables, their equipment, and a pile of what looked like dirty laundry in a heap in the front. I recognized jeans, a sweater, even a pair of sandals I swore I'd seen on someone before.

If you thought the kids were bad, you should have seen the mother. . . .

"Um, guys?" Savannah's voice was shaking. "I think they graduated from chimpanzees."

As a group, we drew closer to the remaining cooling stations. As far as I could tell, only one was currently occupied, its gel mattress inflated and the tubes and wires in place.

My feet stopped working. I couldn't bring myself to move closer.

Eric, however, only sped up. By the time he reached the mattress, he was practically sprinting.

He looked down at the body on the table.

"It's Mom!" he screamed. "Gillian! Help me!"

My knees were jelly. My lungs were rocks in my chest. I tried to inhale, but nothing happened. If Mom was on the table, then that meant . . .

Savannah reached the computer terminal and pulled up the warming protocol on the screen. "It's okay. She's just in torpor. Like the chimp."

Eric was ripping the wires and gel pads off our mom. "I've got you, Mom, I've got you. Gillian!"

If Mom was on the table, then that meant . . .

Far in the distance, I heard the rumble of the truck starting up. Somehow, my feet turned. Somehow, my lungs drew breath. The sound of the engine filled my ears as I sprinted back toward the doors. I heard it rev, heard the truck roll away.

"Dad!" I screamed at the top of my lungs. But I knew I was too late. They'd taken him. The Shepherds had taken him away.

"Um, Gillian?" Howard's cry pierced the fog that fell around me. I turned to see him rooting in the dirty laundry. He held up Nate's General Tso's T-shirt. His voice was high-pitched and terrified, his eyes wide. "Gillian? Where's my brother?"

I looked from Savannah, working feverishly at the keyboard of the cooling station, to Eric, his face stricken as he rubbed my mother's frozen hands between his own. And there I stood, alone, as the sound of the truck vanished into the distance.

My dad was gone. We were on our own.

45 11 21 13 22 11 35 45 31 35 51 13 23 . . .

AUTHOR'S NOTE

I've always wanted to live in the future. When I was younger, I loved learning about new technologies or watching demonstrations of inventions that would soon take over the world (like touch screens). In this book, Gillian and her friends have the chance to live in the future for a few days. Most of the things they discover, from drone feeders to robot restaurant hosts either already exist or are just around the corner. Medically induced hypothermia is being used in hospitals around the world to help accident victims, and the space industry is looking into it as a way to keep costs down on long-term flights. Self-driving ski boats are a little way off, but self-driving cars can already be found on the roads. Solar-paneled highways and bike paths exist—are specially programmed sports courts next?

But the future also holds a dark side. There actually has been a mysterious plague affecting honeybees, and no one quite knows what is causing it (though it's probably not the Shepherds or Wi-Fi). Many scientists agree with the Shepherds that we're not doing enough to prepare our society and our planet for a global catastrophe such as a large asteroid strike. And though the real Ham the Astrochimp, who traveled in space in 1961, retired to a zoo in North Carolina to live out his days in comfort with a mate and family (and his remains probably are in New Mexico . . . or the Smithsonian archives), the fate of many research animals is not so rosy. The abandoned chimp research station in this book is, unfortunately, inspired by the true stories of chimpanzees and other primates used for medical testing and then left to die alone with no food or other resources on islands in the Ivory Coast and Liberia.

As we look forward to the marvels that the future will bring, it's important to remember the dangers, and the responsibility we owe to every fellow inhabitant of this Earth.

ACKNOWLEDGEMENTS

I am grateful to my extended family, who took the pressure off when I needed it most, as well as the mysterious properties of a farmhouse on the northern neck of the Rappahannock. Thank you also to Carrie Ryan and Mari Mancusi, who held my hand through the difficult parts, and K. A. Linde, a marvel, who read an early draft. I also appreciate the advice of E. C. Meyers regarding codes and codebreaking; the anecdotes of Elizabeth Traci Babcock, whose close personal experience with workplace campuses of the future inspired both cool and the terrifying parts of Eureka Cove; and the input of Eliot Schrefer, who made sure I didn't embarrass myself with the monkeys. All remaining errors are my own.

Thank you again to the entire team at Balzer+Bray for their support these many years, especially Kristin Rens, who is the model of patience. I am, as ever, in awe of the artistic ability of Vivienne To. Much love to Michael Bourret, for never giving up on me. Last but not least, thanks to all the readers who want to know what happens next with Gillian, Eric, Savannah, Howard, and Nate.

And Dr. Underberg, of course.